THE
LOST
GIRL

R. L. STINE

THE
LOST
GIRL

A FEAR STREET NOVEL

THOMAS DUNNE BOOKS
ST. MARTIN'S GRIFFIN
NEW YORK

This is a work of fiction. All of the characters, organizations, and events portrayed in this novel are either products of the author's imagination or are used fictitiously.

THOMAS DUNNE BOOKS.
An imprint of St. Martin's Press.

THE LOST GIRL. Copyright © 2015 by Parachute Publishing, LLC. All rights reserved. Printed in the United States of America. For information, address St. Martin's Press, 175 Fifth Avenue, New York, N.Y. 10010.

www.thomasdunnebooks.com
www.stmartins.com

The Library of Congress Cataloging-in-Publication Data is available upon request.

ISBN 978-1-250-05163-9 (hardcover)
ISBN 978-1-4668-8565-3 (e-book)

Our books may be purchased in bulk for promotional, educational, or business use. Please contact your local bookseller or the Macmillan Corporate and Premium Sales Department at (800) 221-7945, extension 5442, or by e-mail at MacmillanSpecialMarkets@macmillan.com.

First Edition: September 2015

10 9 8 7 6 5 4 3 2 1

For Karen Feldgus
Beware of hungry horses

PROLOGUE

SHADYSIDE—1950

1.

What I remember most about that afternoon was the shimmering scarlet and yellow of the sky, as if the heavens were lighting up to join our family's celebration. The sunlight sparkled off the two-day-old snow at the curb, as if someone had piled diamonds in the street.

I think I remember everything about that day.

Running all the way home on the slushy sidewalks from my weekend job at the Clean Bee Laundry. The smell of the dry cleaning and the starch still on my clothes and my skin. I remember the blood thrumming at my temples as I ran and the feeling that, if I raised my arms high, I could take off, lift off from the crowded sidewalks of the Old Village, and glide easily into the pulsating colors of the sky.

I'm very sensitive to colors and light. The silver moonlight has special powers over me. And sunlight fills me with life. Sometimes I can actually feel an electrical charge coursing through my body.

Today was such a happy day for the Palmieri family.

I remember thinking about my grandparents, Mary and Mario, such a perfect couple even their names almost matched. They had come to the United States from Italy in their twenties and worked hard their whole lives to start a new life and bring up a family here.

What a shame they hadn't lived to see this day, my father, Angelo Palmieri, their oldest son, his proudest moment. To go from stable boy to owning his own riding stable. We all couldn't have been more proud.

My parents had been giddy for weeks. I'd catch them giggling and nodding to each other, wide smiles on their normally somber faces.

"What are you two giggling about?" I asked.

"We're just happy, Beth," Dad said. "The closing date on the stable is almost here. Why shouldn't we be happy?"

I can't tell you how good it made me feel to see them so bright and cheerful. Our life wasn't easy. The Dooley family was never generous to my father. They owned the Dooley Brothers Ranch, the big riding stable in North Hills.

As a teenager, Dad had worked there as a stable boy. He returned to the stable after two years at a community college. Eventually, he worked his way up to assistant manager. But the Dooleys ran the place as if they were kings and he was their servant.

They never let him forget that he started out with a shovel in his hand. Martin Dooley, the stable owner, was always reminding Dad how grateful he should be, how he'd be nothing without the Dooleys' generosity.

This made today, the opening of Palmieri Stables, even more exciting. A victory. Not just a success story but a triumph over the Dooleys.

"Dad, does this mean we're going to be rich?" I'd asked at dinner last week. I pictured some new sweaters in my drawer. Maybe one of those cute new 45 record players you can carry with you. Perhaps I could quit my after-school job at the dry cleaner's.

Mom passed the salad bowl. "Beth, you're sixteen," she said. "You should know better than to ask a question like that."

I rolled my eyes and stuck out my jaw. "Should I?"

Mom and I weren't getting along last week. She made me miss a school sock hop dance and a Patti Page concert at the Shadyside Pavilion just because I got a D on a geometry final.

Everyone knows girls aren't good at math. Why does Mom expect me to be so special?

"I want to get married and be a housewife like you, Mom," I said. "Why do I need geometry to do that?"

Mom frowned at me. Her dark eyes appeared to grow hard, like she was sending a Flash Gordon ray beam into my brain. "You don't need geometry to be a housewife," Beth," she said softly. "But you need to be smart."

Ouch.

I had an impulse to make Mom's dinner plate float up into the air and smash on the ceiling above her head.

But my parents don't know about my powers. I call them

my "tricks," and they're my little secret. And I plan to keep them a secret because Mom and Dad already think I'm a problem child.

Dad jumped up from the table and turned on the radio. He doesn't like it when Mom and I have our scenes. "President Truman is giving a talk tonight," he said. "Did you know he started out as a farmer?"

"Oh, no, Dad," I said sarcastically. "You've never told us that before. Except for maybe a thousand times. How a farmer became President of the United States."

Mom stood up, folding her napkin, and began collecting the dinner dishes. "Listen to you, Angelo. You want to be the first stable boy to become president?"

When Dad laughs, his black mustache bounces up and down. "Only if I could bring the horses with me," he said. His smile was reflected in the yellow glow of the radio dial of the big Philco, his proudest possession.

That was a week ago. Now, Mom and I were friends again.

When we walk arm in arm down the street, a lot of people say we look like sisters. We are both thin and about five-six, and have dark, serious eyes and straight black hair. I take it as a compliment when people say we look alike because I think she's prettier than I am. I think my lips are crooked and too big, and my chin is too small.

But anyway, she stopped rattling my cage, and we're pals again.

And it's a great day for the Palmieri family. Opening day.

The snow shoveled off the walks and paths. The stables all freshly painted, the stalls blanketed with straw, and bags of oats stacked up for the first four-legged arrivals. Dad said the newspaper might send a reporter because it's the first new stable-opening in Shadyside since the Dooley's opened theirs nearly forty years ago.

My scarf flew behind me as I darted between people on the street, trotting like a Thoroughbred. Despite the wintry cold, my coat was open. My breath puffed up in front of me, my heart thumping, eager to get to our apartment.

I knew my parents were waiting for me there. Dad had borrowed a station wagon from Mr. Shaw down the block to carry us to the stable.

A tall, skinny black dog tied to a lamppost barked at me as I passed. I nearly stumbled over two boys in plaid snowsuits dragging Flexible Flyer sleds behind them.

I turned the corner onto Village Road—and uttered a sharp cry as two hands grabbed me around the waist. My shoes slid on the slushy sidewalk. The hands held tight, kept me from falling.

"Hey—!" I spun around and gasped. "Aaron! Let go of me."

Heart still pounding in surprise, I blinked into the sunlight and stared at Aaron Dooley's smirking face. Aaron had a red-and-blue wool cap pulled down over his long, straggly black hair. Despite the cold, his face was marshmallow white, like a vampire who had never seen sunlight. His blue eyes glowed like marbles stuck in ice.

I didn't like Aaron Dooley. Actually, I hated him.

But that didn't stop him from pursuing me. I'd told him a dozen times this girl wasn't interested. But he's so smug and conceited, he thought I was just playing hard to get.

He was in a lot of my classes at Shadyside High. And he'd stare at me from across the room and make kissing sounds and flash that thin-lipped smile at me that, I suppose, was supposed to make my heart melt. Instead, it turned my stomach.

I tried to squirm free, but his gloved hands were inside my open coat and he tightened them around my waist.

"Aaron, get off," I snapped. "Get your paws off me. I'm in a hurry."

The icy blue eyes flashed with excitement. He tightened his grip and pulled me to the side of the apartment building. "I'm tired of playing games with you," he said. He always speaks in a gruff growl. I think he's trying to be like John Wayne in the movies.

"There's no game, Aaron," I said. "I told you. I want you to leave me alone." I squirmed again but couldn't free myself. "Come on. I'm really in a hurry."

He pulled me forward and pressed his cold cheek against mine. "You have to give me a chance, Beth."

"No, I don't," I said. The touch of his skin made my stomach lurch. "Let go of me. Go away. I mean it. I'm not interested—"

A frightening roar escaped his throat. His pale face darkened to red, and his lips pulled back tight, as if he was baring his teeth like an animal.

"I won't go away!" he screamed through his gritted teeth. He shoved me off balance. I stumbled. His hands grabbed my arms roughly, and he jerked me forward.

"Aaron—" My breath caught in my throat. "No—!"

He pulled me into the deep shade of the small park between the two buildings. Actually just a snow-covered empty lot with two tall trees near the street.

The snow had hardened to ice here, and my shoes slid as he pulled me behind a wide-trunked tree. He was breathing hard, wheezing, his breath steaming up in front of his glowing blue eyes. His face was crazy, out-of-control crazy.

"You have to give me a chance. You have to," he murmured, his hot breath in my ear. Then he pushed his face against mine. His lips moved till they found my lips. He pressed them harder, and I felt his teeth.

I swung my head back, but he held me in his grasp and pushed his mouth over my lips, forcing me to kiss him. And then he gave a hard shove. Knocked me off balance My shoes slid. I fell to the ice-hard ground on my back.

And before I could move, Aaron was on top of me. He held down my arms and spread his legs over my body. He lowered his head and began frantically planting kisses on my cheeks.

"No! Please!" I screamed. "Aaron—get off me! Get *off* me!"

2.

He didn't stop. Sitting on top of me, he pressed my arms to the ground. His lips felt hot and hard on my face. I knew I wasn't strong enough to shove him away.

I knew I had to act. I had no choice. I had to use my powers. I shut my eyes. I concentrated hard. I said the words to myself. Repeated them silently.

After a few seconds, Aaron's angry, desperate kisses stopped. I opened my eyes. I watched him sit up abruptly, his eyes wide with surprise. And panic.

He let go of my arms and raised his hands to his throat. A sick gagging sound erupted from his mouth. And then he uttered a choking animal wheeze when he realized he couldn't breathe. His eyes bulged. His face darkened to a deep scarlet.

"Why, Aaron," I said. "You seem to have swallowed your tongue. How did that happen?"

He slid off me. Climbed to his knees on the ground. His hands slapped furiously at his throat. He made that disgusting wheezing sound as he struggled to get air. His eyes pleaded with me. They begged me to do something to help him.

But I was enjoying the moment too much to interrupt it. "You deserve it," I said. "You know you deserve it." I climbed to my feet and stood over him, watching his face turn purple, watching him wheeze and gag. His arms flailed helplessly. He groaned and made loud frog croaks. I could see his fat pink tongue curled in his gaping mouth.

"Poor guy," I said with mock sympathy. "That must feel terrible. You can't breathe at all, can you?"

He shook his head. His whole body shuddered. He snapped off a glove and dug his fingers into his open mouth, struggling to pull his tongue back into place. But it was jammed deep in his throat, smothering his windpipe.

He was weakening. His wheezes came more slowly now. His skin was nearly sky blue. He raised both hands to me, pleading.

"Okay, okay," I said. "Would you like me to pull your tongue back out?"

He nodded. His head slumped. He was running out of air.

"Raise your hand," I ordered him. "Raise your right hand and swear you'll never touch me again."

I waited a few seconds. Finally, he found the strength to raise his hand. He groaned. His eyes rolled up in his head.

Had I waited too long?

I bent down, reached my fingers into his mouth, and tugged the tongue back where it should be.

He didn't move. I waited. After a few seconds, Aaron's chest heaved. His eyes slid open and he noisily sucked in breath after breath. His face slowly regained its color. His eyes stared straight ahead, gazing at the tree trunk. He blinked hard, trying to focus. He kept rubbing his throat.

I stood over him, buttoning my coat, enjoying the fear in his eyes.

Yes, Aaron Dooley, the great Martin Dooley's nephew, was afraid of me. I felt like laughing, but I was still too angry to laugh.

Finally, he began breathing normally. Still on his knees on the ground, he raised his eyes to me, and his expression turned angry. "Witch!" he whispered, shaking a finger at me in the air. "Witch! You're a witch!"

Now, I couldn't help myself. I tossed back my head and laughed. I guess that's what witches are supposed to do. Then I turned away, kicking snow onto him, and took off for home.

3.

I burst into the door of our apartment just in time to leave for the stable opening ceremonies. My parents and my cousins already had coats on and were standing by the door at attention.

Mom eyed me, then glanced down at her watch. "Beth, how can you be late on your father's big day?" she said.

"I'll tell you why I'm late!" I cried. "I was almost home. Aaron Dooley grabbed me and wouldn't let me go. He dragged me into an empty lot, forced me to the ground, and attacked me. But I used one of my tricks. I made him swallow his tongue. I think Aaron will behave from now on. But he's the reason I'm late."

Did I say that to my Mom?

Of course not.

One, my parents don't know anything about my little tricks. And, two, why would I spoil the big day? This was our family's biggest celebration. If I told them about how Aaron had attacked me, my dad would go into a fist-pumping screaming rage, my mom would start crying, and the whole day would be ruined.

So . . . I kept my mouth shut. I shrugged and said, "Sorry. They kept me late at the laundry. I ran all the way home."

That seemed to satisfy Mom. She moved to the mirror and adjusted the fox's head on the fox stole around her neck.

I hugged my cousins David and Mariana. Peter, their four-year-old son, hid behind Mariana, his arms around her legs, and wouldn't say hi to me. He's very shy.

"Where's Aunt Hannah?" I asked.

"We're picking her up on the way," Dad said. He pulled a tan fedora down over his balding head, a hat that had to be new because I'd never seen it before. It had a red-and-yellow feather in the band and a much wider brim than Dad usually wears. Fancy.

He wore his only suit, black and shiny, a little too shiny, single-breasted with the wide lapels. I always told him it made him look like a gangster in the movies. You know. Al Capone or somebody. I think Dad liked that.

Mom dressed up, too, in the satiny red dress she wears to parties and baptisms, and at Christmas. She looked very pretty with her black hair piled up, held in place with a rhinestone headband.

It was a big day, and everyone knew it. And everyone was talking at the same time as we squeezed into Mr. Shaw's station wagon, "This car is almost brand-new," Dad said, squeezing his big overcoat behind the wheel. "It's a 1948 model." He was bragging about it as if he owned it. "A Packard Commodore. Plenty of room."

I sat between Mom and Dad in the front seat as we began the short drive. The stable is on the River Road, on a sloping hill overlooking the Conononka River, about fifteen minutes away.

In the seat behind us, Cousin David made horse-whinnying sounds, trying to get a laugh from Peter. But grumpy as usual, Peter refused to get into the spirit of the day. "Be quiet," he snapped at his dad.

"Do you let him talk to you like that?" Dad said. Dad believes all other parents should be strict. He was always a pushover.

"Your uncle Angelo doesn't like you to talk to me like that," David told his son.

"Be quiet," Peter replied.

David whinnied again. "Know what I'm going to do? I'm going to buy a horse and name it Peter."

"No!" Peter protested.

"Why not?" David teased him. "Then we'll have Peter the Boy and Peter the Horse."

"No! I don't want that!" Peter whined.

David didn't stop teasing the boy. "We'll buy a horse and your uncle Angelo will keep it for us for free, won't you, Angelo?"

My dad pretended to choke. He turned the big station wagon onto the River Road. "I'll keep your horse for free,

David, after I get down on all fours and win the Kentucky Derby."

Everyone thought that was pretty funny.

I stared out the windshield, trying to force myself to get into the party mood. But I couldn't get Aaron Dooley out of my mind. What did he think he was doing? Did he really think he could win me over by dragging me away and attacking me like that?

Ugh. Like some kind of crude prehistoric caveman.

The same questions kept swimming through my mind. Was Aaron totally out of control? How far would he have gone if I hadn't used one of my tricks?

Could I be in real trouble now? Was Aaron Dooley dangerous?

The big station wagon crunched over the long gravel path that led to the stable. I saw the flag flapping hard at the top of the flagpole in the front. Red-white-and-blue banners were draped over the main entrance doors to the horse barn.

A crowd had already gathered. Two kids in blue snowsuits were wrestling in the snow. A photographer in a long gray trench coat had his box camera trained on them.

I recognized six or seven of our cousins. They huddled near the entrance, slapping their gloves together to keep their hands warm. And I saw some of the teachers from the middle school where Mom used to be the librarian.

Dad stopped the car at the end of the gravel driveway, and we piled out. The crowd started to cheer, and Dad took a short bow and raised his new hat to them. He was beaming with pride and happiness.

Enjoy the celebration, Beth, I told myself. *Clear your mind. Stop thinking about Aaron.*

And I was able to do that during the short, happy ceremony. And during my father's speech, thanking everyone for coming and thanking all those who had helped him reach this wonderful day.

When he thanked my mom, I saw tears form in her eyes. She wiped them away quickly with a gloved finger, a trembling smile on her face. Mom would never want anyone to see her be emotional. Then we all enjoyed glasses of champagne or sparkling cider and toasted the new stable.

I was able to relax and enjoy myself and chat with people and keep Aaron Dooley from my mind.

Until Aaron's uncle, Martin Dooley, showed up. And our happy day turned to horror.

4.

I saw Martin Dooley arrive a few minutes after everyone had climbed back into their cars and left for home. Dad had stayed behind in the office to go over a few papers with Mr. Kliner from the bank.

I took a walk through the horse barn as I waited for Dad to finish. The sweet aroma of fresh straw made me happy, and I imagined the stalls filled with horses.

When I heard the hard *thud* of boots stomping over snow, I peered out the window and saw Martin Dooley walking fast, his purple-gloved fists swinging at his sides.

I held my breath. *What is HE doing here?*

Martin Dooley isn't tall or big or muscular. But he looks powerful and important. It's hard to explain. He isn't very good-looking. He has tiny gray bird eyes the size of marbles, and a turned-up nose, and his lips are practically as pale as his skin. He's in his forties, I think, but he has sharp bristly white hair, cut short in a flattop. His head always reminds me of a hairbrush.

I've never seen him smile.

Dad once said that Martin is like a shark. He never looks from side to side. He just barges forward with his teeth snapping.

He wears very expensive suits that he buys in New York and colorful wide ties with wild flower designs that don't suit his personality at all. And he splashes cologne on his face that makes him smell like a lemon.

Through the barn window, I glimpsed his long black overcoat with a fur-trimmed collar and his polished black boots as he hurried over the snow to the office. At first, I decided to stay in the warmth and safety of the stable. But my curiosity got the better of me, and I crept to the side door where I could overhear the conversation.

The door had a frosted glass window. I stayed back a few feet, eager not to be seen. Through the smoky glass, I watched the blurred image of my dad jump up from his desk. "Martin? What are *you* doing here?" He couldn't hide his surprise.

Martin's heavy boots made the floorboards creak as he crossed the room. "I think you forgot to send me an invitation, Angelo," he said.

His voice is deep, but he always speaks softly, as if holding himself in. His parents came from Ireland, and he speaks with a tiny bit of an Irish accent. Dad says he puts it on because he thinks it's charming.

"Well, I'm very surprised—" Dad started.

"I'm the one who's surprised, don't you know," Martin

interrupted. "I expected gratitude from you, Angelo. Instead I get betrayal."

My dad hesitated. "Betrayal? That's a strong word, Martin. I haven't betrayed anyone, especially you. If you're talking about this stable . . . I . . . I discussed it with you and—"

"And we decided it was a mistake, a bad idea." Martin snickered. "An idea whose time hasn't come."

I clenched my fists. I wanted to shout in protest. I held my breath to keep myself from making a sound. Even through the door, I could feel the tension in that room. Distorted in the frosted window glass, I saw Martin Dooley lean over the desk, bring his face close to my dad, challenging him.

"Angelo, did you really think I could allow this to happen?"

Dad was silent for a moment. "You have no choice," he said sharply. My dad can be tough when he wants to be.

"No choice?" Martin uttered a mirthless laugh. "This stable will not be standing in a year. That's not a prediction. It's a fact."

Dad stood head-to-head with Martin Dooley. "I-I don't think we have anything to say to one another," he stammered. "I think—"

Martin Dooley slammed a fist on the desktop. "Do you really think I will allow a *stable boy* to destroy my business?"

"I think you should leave," Dad insisted. His voice trembled with anger. "I think you should leave. I was your business manager. I ran your business. I've earned a little respect. I'm *not* a stable boy, Martin. Perhaps you need eyeglasses. I'm not—"

"And how can you explain your daughter?" Martin suddenly changed the subject.

I gasped and took a step back from the door. Did he see me? Is that why he mentioned me?

My dad sputtered in surprise. "Explain?"

"My nephew Aaron tells me she keeps rejecting him. Does Beth really think she's too good to go out with a Dooley?" Martin boomed. "You've put some bad ideas in her head, Angelo. Bad ideas. Your daughter is very confused. But don't worry. My nephew Aaron will teach her what's what."

Dad had remained in control. But now he began to shout. "Why are you talking about Beth? Why do you bring up my daughter? Your worthless nephew isn't going to teach her anything. Get out of here, Martin. You have no business talking about my daughter. You have no business—"

"You're a stable boy, Angelo!" Martin screamed back at him. "You're a stable boy. You belong with a shovel in your hands. Only, you know what? I think you're not *good* enough to shovel what my horses leave on the ground. You need to be taught—"

Martin never finished the sentence. I heard a hard *thwack*. I gasped as I realized my dad had punched him.

Martin's cry rang off the bare stable walls.

My hand trembled as I pulled the door open a little wider. My heart was racing, beating so hard my chest ached.

Martin Dooley's head was lowered. He rubbed his jaw. He raised his face slowly. His cheeks were scarlet, his eyes watery pools.

My dad stood behind the desk with his fist still clenched. Beneath his open suit jacket, Dad's chest was heaving up and down.

Martin bent to pick his hat up off the floor. Still rubbing his jaw, he narrowed his eyes in a cold, menacing stare. "I'll be back, stable boy," he said softly. "You've made a big mistake."

It wasn't an empty threat. Two days later, my family paid for the punch Dad had landed on Martin Dooley's jaw.

Two days later, my life ended.

5.

The first horses were to arrive at our stable that night. In the afternoon, Dad held a meeting of his workers, six of them in all, to discuss assignments.

I was there because the boiler had broken at Shadyside High and the school was closed. Dad gave me a job. He had dozens of reins and harnesses tangled together in a big wooden crate. He asked me to pull them out and untangle them.

I was halfway through the crate when Dad ended the staff meeting. They all hurried to their cars to take a short break before the horses arrived and things would get crazy.

A bunch of black leather reins were tangled together like snakes. I was leaning over the crate, working on them with both hands when I heard a car pull up on the gravel drive. Curious, I pulled myself up straight and crossed to the office door.

I gasped as two men in large black overcoats burst noisily into the office. I blinked several times. I didn't really believe what I was seeing. Their faces were hidden. They had black wool masks over their faces, their wide-brimmed hats pulled low.

Startled, Dad jumped up from behind the desk. "What—?"

The two men rushed forward and grabbed him roughly by the arms.

Dad twisted and squirmed and tried to free himself. They struggled. "What is this? Is this a robbery? I don't have any money here. What do you think you're doing?" He managed to pull one arm free. But a masked man grabbed it and twisted it hard behind Dad's back.

Dad let out a sharp cry. "You . . . You're breaking my arm! What is this about? What are you doing?"

"We have a surprise from Martin Dooley," one of them rasped.

I almost cried out when he gave Dad a sharp blow on the back of the neck with his open hand. Dad groaned and his head slumped forward. His shoes scraped the floor as the two men dragged him to the door.

I didn't move. I couldn't breathe. I stood staring with every muscle in my body tensed and tight, as if I'd been tied up with rope.

This isn't happening. I didn't really believe it. This kind of thing happened only in the movies, right?

Halfway to the door, Dad groaned again, and one of the men gave him another hard punch in the back of the neck. Dad's head jerked back, then fell forward. His arms fell limp over the overcoat shoulders of the two men as they dragged him.

When the door slammed hard behind them, the sound finally shocked me out of my stupor. I staggered into the now-empty office, gasping for breath. A flood of questions washed over me. *Where are they taking him? What are they going to do? What should I do?*

My eyes glimpsed Dad's car keys on the edge of his desk. I realized I had to follow them. *I can help him. I know I can. I HAVE to help him.* I swiped the keys off the desk, my hand cold and wet.

I stumbled to the door, my heart racing. I knew I had to calm down. My whole body was shaking. My head was throbbing. I kept hearing Dad's groan of pain when the man punched him.

I can't drive unless I calm down. I need to think straight. I've got to overcome this panic.

I'd never felt anything like this. We all have moments of fear, I guess. But total paralyzing panic was something I never dreamed I'd experience.

You have your tricks, Beth. Remember, you have powers.

The thought gave me a little reassurance, enough to start breathing again, enough for my head to stop throbbing as if it was ready to burst apart.

Through the office window, I saw the two men heave Dad into the backseat of their long black sedan. The afternoon sun was setting behind the trees. Long shadows spread over their car as it squealed backward, spun hard, then shot down the gravel drive.

Taking deep breaths, fighting the panic away, I waited till they were out of sight. Then I bolted out the door and ran to our little Ford, my shoes sinking into the wet snow. The burst of cold air sent a shiver down my body, but it helped revive me. I dropped behind the wheel and fumbled the key into the ignition.

"Please start. Please start," I begged the car. The car had bad habits, like not starting the first four or five tries. I pulled out the choke, turned the key, and stepped down on the gas pedal. The car coughed once, twice, then the engine started with a roar.

I turned the car and gunned the engine. The tires spun on the slick surface, and the car began to slide. Dad had been talking about getting new tires for ages. These were worn down to the hubcaps. I worked the wheel furiously until the tires took hold, and then I headed the car down the hill, determined to follow the thugs who had kidnapped my dad.

I didn't expect so much traffic on the River Road. People driving home from work. I turned a little too hard and nearly rear-ended a red Mercury. The driver blasted his horn at me. I eased my foot off the brake and took another deep, shuddering breath.

You can do this, Beth. You've got to help your father.

I could see the black sedan three or four cars ahead of

me. I wondered if I could keep it in sight. But when their car turned onto Park Drive and headed in the direction of North Hills, I knew where they were going. I didn't need them to show the way.

They were heading to the Dooley Stable.

The offices and staff building, the barn and stables, the supply house and other outbuildings of the Dooley stable face each other and form a wide square. The riding paths lead into the Fear Street Woods, which stretches behind the huge barn. In the middle of the four buildings is a courtyard big enough to hold dressage and equestrian contests.

The snow had been cleared from the wide asphalt driveway that leads to the parking lot beside the staff building. I pulled the Ford two-thirds of the way up the drive, just close enough to see the parking lot. The black sedan was parked at an angle next to the building. Squinting into the dying sunlight, I could see that the car was empty.

"Dad, where did they take you?" I murmured out loud.

I shut off the ignition. My car was safely out of view, I decided. I climbed out, my breath steaming up in front of me.

I gasped when I heard the scream. I thought it was my dad. But it was only the high whinny of a horse from the long line of stalls.

I let out a long *whoosh* of air. Forced my heartbeat to slow. My eyes scanned the parking lot and the front of the staff building. No one in sight.

My shoes sinking into the snow, I started to make my way toward the staff building. I kept under the shadow of the trees that lined the driveway.

Where did they take him? What do they plan to do to him? Am I in time?

I ducked against the wall at the side of the building. Long silvery icicles, like shiny sword blades, hung down from the gutter over my head. I moved forward keeping my back against the wall and studied the front entrance.

Should I risk it? Go in the front entrance and search for him in the staff offices?

I hesitated. I took a few steps toward the front doors, then stopped when I heard voices. Men's voices. They seemed to be coming from the courtyard behind the building.

The sun had started to melt the snow, leaving a slippery, slushy layer on top. I half-walked, half-slid as I made my way to the courtyard. Purple evening sunlight washed over the ground.

When I saw my dad, between the two masked men, I almost called out to him. He struggled to free himself, but they held tightly to his shoulders. His hands were tied behind him. He stumbled and nearly fell, but the two thugs held him up.

I took a few steps closer, squinting into the hazy gray light. *Oh, no.* Dad was in his underwear. They had stripped his clothes off him. He was in a sleeveless undershirt and white boxer shorts. He was barefoot. Walking barefoot in the snow.

He shouted and cursed at his two captors. He lowered a shoulder and tried to butt one of them to the side. The man's boot tromped down hard on Dad's bare foot, and Dad groaned in pain.

I saw two low stakes poking up from the snow. The men shoved Dad to the ground. They had coils of rope. They prepared to tie him down to the stakes.

"Please—" Dad was begging now. "Please—let me go. What are you doing? This is crazy. You know this isn't right. Let me go. I won't call the police. I won't say anything. Just let me go." He was pleading in a voice I'd never heard, a trembling stream of words.

One man shoved Dad onto his back in the snow and held him in place. The other man tugged at the ropes around Dad's hands and started to tie his hands to one of the stakes.

"What are you doing? Are you going to leave me in the snow? You know this is murder. Do you really—"

The man let go of the rope and back-handed Dad across the face. Dad's head snapped to the side. The man turned and went back to tying Dad to the stake.

Why am I standing here? I asked myself. *Why am I watching them preparing to let my dad freeze to death in the snow?*

I knew I had to act.

"Let me go! Let me go!" Dad's frightened cries rang out around the courtyard. Horses began to whinny. Their shrill cries drowned out my father's pleas. The bleats of the horses echoed off the buildings, the sound rising until it became deafening, a blaring animal symphony of fright, of terror.

I covered my ears, but I couldn't shut out the shrill whinnying. I struggled to breathe. I could feel the blood pulsing at my temples.

I have powers. Time to use them.

I shut my eyes. I murmured the words I had memorized long ago. Murmured the words and repeated them rapidly. Kept my eyes shut tight, seeing nothing, forcing away all images, murmuring in a soft whisper, repeating the words, urging the spell to work quickly.

Again, I heard my dad's terrified cries. Again, the bleats of the horses drowned him out. I heard the crash of horses kicking their stall walls. A burst of icy wind blew through the courtyard.

I murmured the words . . . whispered . . . repeating them again . . . again. Then in the rushing wind with the horses kicking and crying, I opened my eyes to see what I had done—and gasped in horror.

6.

I squinted in the gray light. Dad, on his back, kicked and thrashed. His hands were stretched over his head, tied to the stake. The two men bent over him, working to tie his feet to the other stake.

I let out a long sigh. *My spell hadn't worked.* Was it because I was so scared, too frightened to summon the magic I had learned?

The men suddenly looked up. I pressed myself flat against the wall of the building. I held my breath. My head throbbed. The magic always started my brain spinning.

Why didn't my spell work?

Dad screamed for help. His scream made the horses start up their cries again. The two men left him on his back. They both trudged toward the supply building, their boots crunching loudly over the snow.

I pushed away from the wall and took a few steps toward my dad. But then I stopped. I knew I probably couldn't get him untied before the men returned. And if I was captured, too, I wouldn't be able to use my tricks to save him.

So I forced myself to stay out of sight. And I watched as the two men came marching back, each carrying a large brown can. Gallon cans of . . . what?

"What are you *doing*?" Dad screamed as they tilted the cans over him and a thick golden liquid oozed out. "Gasoline? Huh? Gasoline? Are you going to set me on fire?"

"Relax, Angelo. Do we look like the kind of men who would set you on fire?" the taller one said, pouring the liquid over the front of my dad's undershirt.

"What is it? Tell me. What is it?" Dad demanded.

"It's honey," the other thug said. "Sweet honey. Look how sweet you are."

They both laughed. They poured the honey over my dad's legs, his chest. They emptied the cans over him, then tossed them across the courtyard. They gazed down at him, seemingly pleased with their work.

This is insane, I thought. *What are they planning?*

I shut my eyes again. I had to make the magic work. I had to stop this whole thing now. But the words wouldn't come to me. The words were lost, hiding somewhere in my fevered brain.

I clenched my fists in frustration. I opened my eyes—in time to see the taller masked man holding a big burlap bag over my dad. "Oats," he said. "We can't forget the oats, can we?"

He tore open the bag. His partner helped him hold it

up. They tilted it and emptied the oats onto my dad. They covered his chest, his waist, his legs.

Dad had gone silent. He stopped squirming and twisting. His bare arms and legs were red from the cold. Now he lay still, under the oats, stuck to him in the honey. From where I stood, it looked as if he had a brown blanket spread over him.

"I . . . I don't understand," he said to the two men in a soft voice, just above a whisper. He sounded defeated. The fight had gone out of him. "What are you doing? I don't understand."

"You want to feed the horses, don't you, Angelo?" the taller one said.

"Yeah, you *like* feeding the horses," his partner chimed in. "It'll be like old times."

"No. Wait—" My dad pleaded.

"The horses are starving," the taller one said. "They haven't been fed in days."

"No. Please—" My dad had figured out what they planned to do, and so had I.

They were going to let the hungry horses out of their stalls so they could come feed on the oats spread over my father.

I started to picture their lowered heads, their gnashing teeth as they chomped hungrily into my dad's chest. *No!* I forced the picture from my mind.

I shut my eyes and frantically struggled to remember the words of my spell. But no. They wouldn't come. They were lost. My panic had chased the words from my memory. And now . . .

I opened my eyes and saw someone trotting across the snow. The two men turned to greet him. Aaron. Aaron Dooley. His red-and-black plaid coat was open, revealing a black sweater underneath. He had a red wool cap pulled down over his long hair.

Oh, thank goodness, I thought. For the moment, I forgot about my violent encounter with him two days earlier. And I felt glad to see him as he jogged toward my father's captors.

You'll stop this, won't you, Aaron? I thought.

You'll stop this. You won't let this happen—right?

7.

As I watched holding my breath, silently praying for Aaron to do something, he trotted up to the two masked men, his breath streaming up above his head. He crossed his arms and gazed down at my dad. He said something to the men that I couldn't hear.

I leaned forward from the corner of the building, begging, pleading. *Please, Aaron. Please.*

He turned. Did he see me? I snapped my head back out of sight.

When I gathered the courage to look again, I saw that the two masked men had moved to the barn. They began opening stall doors. Aaron didn't move, just stood there with his arms crossed, his back to my father.

The horses came *screaming* out of the stalls. Their hooves thundered on the snow, their heads tossed back, their voices raised in a siren-like whistle, a deafening, desperate cry. Their eyes were wild. They rose up on their back legs and whinnied at the sky.

My dad's scream rose over the horse's whinnies as they attacked him. They galloped in a line, lowered their heads, bared enormous teeth, and began to chew. Grunting, snapping their teeth, hoofing at him, kicking him, they voraciously devoured the oats, ripping at his body, their teeth tearing chunks of skin away as they frantically fed.

Dad's screams of agony rose with the cries and shrieks of the horses. They pawed him, bit and chewed into his flesh, into his chest, his arms. Blood spurted into the air and puddled on the snow.

Dad's screams stopped. I saw his arms go limp. His head fell back, as if he couldn't bear to watch any more of it.

And still the horses grunted and chewed, tearing Dad apart, tearing his skin off, hungrily swallowing, digging their big teeth deeper . . . deeper into his body.

Paralyzed by fear, I couldn't bear to watch—but I couldn't look away. I felt like I was outside myself, not in my body at all, watching something impossible, something that could never happen.

But my dad's unmoving silence . . . the lake of dark blood around him in the snow . . . the chunks of flesh scattered on the ground . . . it snapped me out of my dream state. Was I too late to get help?

Probably.

But I had to find someone. Without thinking, I ran from the safety of the building. My idea was to try to find help in the staff building. But in my shock and horror, and with the living nightmare of seeing my father eaten by horses, I lurched the wrong way.

Before I could pull back, I heard one of the men shout, "Hey—look! It's his daughter!"

I gasped. And heard the other masked man yell, "Don't let her get away. The horses are still hungry."

8.

I didn't turn back. I lowered my head and ran straight past them.

"We don't need a witness," one of the men shouted. And then I heard the rapid *thud* of footsteps over the now. I glanced back and saw Aaron chasing after me, his open coat flapping behind him, his cold blue eyes narrowed in determination.

"Noooo . . . ." I gasped. I darted around the back of the barn building and followed the riding path that led into the Fear Street Woods. The snow was piled higher back here. No one had shoveled. The wind had blown drifts nearly to my knees.

"Beth—stop!" Aaron called. "You know you can't outrun me."

I jumped over a fallen tree limb, ducked my head under some snow-covered brambles, and plunged into the woods.

Behind me, Aaron uttered a cry. I turned to see him fall

over the tree limb. He picked himself up quickly, brushing snow off the front of his black sweater.

A wind shuddered the trees, and snow fell off the branches. I lowered my head and kept running.

"Beth! Beth! Beth!" he kept chanting my name as he came after me.

Did he think I'd turn around to answer him? Did he think I'd ever speak to him after . . . after . . .

A low branch scratched my face. I cried out in pain, spun away and headed along a patch of tall shrubs that led downhill.

Aaron's calls suddenly seemed farther away. Was he falling behind?

Maybe I can outrun him.

I leaned forward and tried to pick up speed. But I was running downhill and my shoes landed on a square patch of ice on top of the snow. I started to slide, my arms flailing at my sides, struggling to keep my balance.

As I started to go down, I wrapped my arms around the trunk of a slender birch tree, spun around the tree, and came to a stop.

Panting hard, I listened for Aaron. No footsteps. No cries. Had I managed to lose him in my frantic dash through these tangled woods?

Both of my sides throbbed with pain. I couldn't slow my racing heartbeats. I glanced around quickly. I had no idea where I was. No idea how to find my way out of the woods.

A row of white-trunked birch trees stood on my right.

To my left, a snowy path cut through scraggly shrubs and reeds. I took the path, forcing my legs to move, ignoring the pains in my sides. Had I already been this way? I couldn't remember.

I kept glancing back, searching for Aaron. Did I lose him? Was he still coming after me?

I've got to get out of the woods. But—how?

I came to the end of the path, turned to see where I was—and ran right into Aaron.

"HA!" he uttered a triumphant laugh. He wrapped his arms around my waist and tightened his grip. "Did you think you lost me?"

"Aaron—let me go," I choked out. "Why are you doing this? They're going to *kill* me. Is that what you *want*?"

I didn't give him a chance to answer. I shot my knee up as hard as I could into the pit of his stomach. His eyes bulged and he let out a groan. His arms slid off me, and he dropped to his knees in the snow, gasping in pain.

I didn't give him time to recover. Kicking snow as I ran, I took off to a thick clump of low-limbed trees up ahead. The tree limbs were bent, many of them nearly to the ground. I ducked my head and stumbled forward, eager to lose myself behind the tangle of limbs.

Where does this lead?

To my surprise, the trees ended at the mouth of a low cave cut into gray rock. I ducked under the last tree limb and darted into the cave. The air felt a lot colder inside.

I made my way a few feet into the cave, then turned

back. Had Aaron seen me? He couldn't be far behind. If he came running through the clump of tangled tree limbs, he'd see the cave, and he'd know . . . he'd know . . .

I backed in farther. Backed into a deep well of black. The cave was longer than I'd imagined. The air grew even colder . . . and heavier. The heavy chill made me shudder.

Please . . . please don't find me.

I gasped. It felt as if whirls of darkness were circling me, washing over me . . . pulling me down, forcing me deeper into the cave. Swallowed. I was being swallowed by the inky darkness. I suddenly couldn't breathe. I couldn't move. I felt myself sinking into the shadows . . . shadows over shadows . . . shadows rolling and dancing over shadows.

I was falling helplessly into a darkness I'd never seen before. And as I fell, I knew I was fading, fading, fading away . . .

Is this what it feels like to die?

PART
ONE

PRESENT DAY

9.

Michael? Michael Frost!"

I looked up from my phone when I heard my name called. I'd been staring at a text from Pepper Davis, my girlfriend, trying to decide if it made any sense or not. Pepper likes to send texts with no whole words, only bunches of letters like OMG or LMAO and then a string of emojis. I was never good at languages. You can ask Mr. LeForet, my French teacher. The other day, it took me twenty minutes to decipher a text from Pepper that said: *I'll meet you after school at your house.*

"Hey, Michael!"

I lowered the phone, turned, and saw a guy at the end of the dairy section, grinning at me. I didn't recognize him at first. He must have been a little older than me, early twenties I'd guess. His hair was shaved short on the sides, and he wore a maroon and yellow sweatshirt that said WORLD TOUR 09 on the front, pulled down over baggy cargo khakis.

He shifted the shopping basket he held in one hand and stepped toward me. "Hey, it's me. Buddy Griffman. Remember? I was an intern at your dad's store a few winters ago?"

"Hey, yeah," I said. "How's it going?"

"It's going okay." He gestured to the shopping basket. I saw a big pack of Pampers and several cans of something called Similac. "Got a kid now." He flashed me a strange grin, like he was embarrassed or something. "No more interning, you know?"

I nodded. My phone dinged but I ignored it. Probably another unreadable text from Pepper. "Where you working, Buddy?"

He shrugged. "Sort of in-between things, you know. Staying with my parents in Martinsville." He shifted his weight. "How's your dad? How's his business? Good, right? This winter . . ."

I nodded. "Well, there's been a ton of snow. That's good for snowmobiles, you know. Dad's probably the only guy in town who prays for *more* snow every winter."

Buddy tossed back his head and laughed. A little too hard. It wasn't that funny. Then we had an awkward moment where neither one of us knew what to say next.

I waved my phone. "I've got to . . . uh . . . answer this. . . ."

"Michael, tell your dad I said hi." He shifted the basket to his other hand and headed down the aisle. He was wearing sandals even though there was about eight inches of snow on the ground outside.

I don't remember this guy at all, I thought. *Did I ever meet him?*

I moved my cart in the other direction. I had the chicken breasts and the vegetables Mom needed. Now I had to find black olives. Don't ask. Some kind of new chicken/olive thing Mom was whipping up for dinner tonight.

I shop for her here at the Food Mart all the time. I'm not the best shopper in the world. In fact, I suck at it. But Mom works two jobs, so I don't mind pitching in.

I spotted a likely shelf across from the cold cuts counter. I had to swerve my cart around a middle-aged bald guy in gray sweats who was balancing a whole ham in each hand. He had the two hams raised above his head. At first, I thought maybe he was *working out* with them. Cheaper than the gym, right? Then I realized he was showing them to his wife at the end of the aisle.

I rolled my cart past the cold cuts shelves, and that's when I spotted the girl.

She was . . . beautiful. Well . . . not drop-dead beautiful. But there was something unreal about her, something startling that made me stand there staring at her.

I'm really into writing. Pepper and I write a Shadyside High blog every day. And I plan to be an English major when I start at Duke next fall.

But it would take a better writer than me to describe this

girl. What was it about her that was so totally fascinating? I guess it was her eyes. She had big, glowing cat eyes. Like that movie star. What's her name? Emma Stone? Big, beautiful eyes, only black. Against her pale face, they looked like shimmering black olives. Ha. Yeah, I had olives on my mind.

She had black hair that fell down the sides of her face in tight curls. She didn't smile. Actually, she looked troubled. Her lips were together in a kind of pout. She wore a black hoodie with the hood pushed back, over straight-legged denim jeans.

"Excuse me, please. Excuse me." A woman wanted to move her cart past me. She had to ask three times before I realized she was talking to me. Like I was in a trance or something.

I rolled my cart to the side. I turned back to the girl. She still hadn't noticed me. Her eyes were on the cold cut packages.

I took a few steps toward her. I'm not sure why. It was like an invisible force was pulling me to her. But I stopped when I saw her raise her large purple canvas bag.

Her eyes darted from right to left. Then she quickly grabbed up packs of ham and turkey and shoved them into her bag.

I blinked. *This isn't happening, is it?*

It took only a few seconds. She closed the bag, tucked the handle under her arm, and moved slowly, casually to the bread department. I followed her. I couldn't help it. I watched her tuck a small loaf of crusty bread into her bag.

Her face was expressionless. Her eyes were blank. She smiled as she passed two white-aproned store workers. I watched her walk slowly through the automatic exit door and into the parking lot.

No one chased after her. No one had seen her steal the food. But me.

Why did I follow her? Why did I leave my cart in the middle of the aisle and hurry out the door after her?

I don't know. I guess I thought maybe I could help her. I mean, I wasn't going to turn her in. I didn't plan to try to stop her. I thought maybe she needed help—and why wouldn't I try to help such a totally hot, mysterious-looking girl?

Some of my friends say I'm a do-gooder. They call me Scout. You know. Like I'm a Boy Scout or something. They think it's funny, but I don't see anything wrong with it.

Maybe she's really poor, and she's hungry, I thought. *Maybe she lost her wallet. Maybe she's run away from home. . . .*

My dog was tied up at the side of the building. She bent to pet the dog, and I caught up with her there. She raised her eyes, saw me for the first time. "Is this your dog?"

I nodded. "Yeah." Suddenly a little speechless.

"What kind of dog?"

"She's a mix," I said. "Mostly Lab."

"Cute. How old?"

"Almost three."

"Still a puppy." She scratched the dog's ears. "What's her name?"

"Mindy," I answered.

She laughed. "Mindy? Really? That's *my* name!" She stood up. She gripped the canvas bag handles tightly. I kept glancing at the bag, picturing her stealing the food.

"No. Seriously," I said. "Your name is Mindy?"

She nodded, a teasing grin on her face. "Yes. I'm Mindy. Mindy Barker."

"Hey," I said. "Barker? Like a dog?"

She had a great giggle.

"Come on. Give me a break. What's your real name?" I asked.

She shrugged. Her big eyes flashed. She enjoyed teasing me. "Mindy Barker is a good name, don't you think?"

If only I could stop picturing her shoplifting. I gazed at the bag. There was no way I could bring it up, say that I saw what she did.

She'd run away.

And I didn't want her to run away.

"I haven't seen you in school," I said. "Do you go to Shadyside?"

"I'm new. I just started."

"Are you a senior, too?"

She tugged at a long, red-plastic earring that dangled from her black hair. "Yeah."

"Must be hard moving to a new school for your senior year," I said.

She rolled her eyes. "Tell me about it." Her expression suddenly changed. "Why do you keep staring at my bag?"

I blinked. "Me? I wasn't. Really." I could feel the blood rushing to my cheeks.

She gave Mindy a final pet. "Gotta run. See you in school, Michael."

She turned and took off, trotting full speed across the wide parking lot. The canvas bag swung heavily at her side.

I stood there beside Mindy, watching the girl run. She didn't look back. She vanished behind the last row of parked cars. "Weird," I muttered. "She is definitely weird, Mindy."

I suddenly remembered my groceries. I made sure Mindy was still tied securely. Then I started back into the store. As the door slid open, a thought burst into my mind:

Hey, how did she know my name?

10.

I saw the girl again the next afternoon at the end of lunch period. My friend Gabe Diller and I finished lunch early. Gabe had a new game on his phone he was desperate to show me. Everyone has a friend who just wants to play games on any screen day and night. In my case, it's Gabe.

He says it's great for his hand-eye coordination. But Gabe doesn't play any sports or anything, so I don't know why he needs hand-eye coordination.

We wandered to the lounge by the front of the library where teachers wouldn't see us. Students are allowed to have phones, but we're not allowed to use them during the day because you know how irresponsible teenagers can be. Ha.

The hall was silent here. Most everyone was still at lunch. Gabe started up the game on his big Android phone. It has a nice-sized screen for playing games, if you're into games. I laughed when I saw it was a snowmobile-racing game.

My dad's store is called Frost's Snowmobile Ranch. He

rents and sells snowmobiles and RVs, and most of his talk at the dinner table every night is about snow and snowmobiles, and sometimes I picture myself living in one of those snow globes. You know. You shake them and the snow floats down. There's no way to escape it!

Gabe tilted his phone, demonstrating how to make the snowmobile go faster. He plunged off a cliff and the snowmobile blasted apart in a fiery crash at the bottom.

Gabe blinked at the screen. "I didn't mean to do that."

"Did you go out with Rachel Martin on Friday?" I asked him.

He squinted at the screen, resetting the game. "Well, we didn't actually go out."

I poked him in the side. "What did you do? Stay home and play *World of Warcraft*?"

He grinned. "How did you guess?" His thumbs furiously worked the controls. The snowmobile roared to life. "I think Rachel was kind of bored."

"So you probably won't see her again?"

"Probably not."

"I thought you *liked* her."

"I do," he replied, eyes on the screen. "She's awesome. But . . . I have a war to fight." He burst out laughing. So did I. We both knew he was being ridiculous.

He shoved the phone into my hand. "Want to try it?"

Before I could answer, I saw the girl. She came walking toward us slowly, her eyes scanning each classroom door. She had a floppy knit cap over her dark hair and wore a gray sweater pulled down over a short straight plaid skirt with black leggings.

"Mindy!" I called to her.

She turned and recognized me.

I saw Gabe's eyes go wide. He studied her as she jogged over to us.

"Hey, Gabe, this is Mindy Barker," I said.

She made a face. "That's not my real name, Michael. That's my dog name."

"What's your cat name?" Gabe asked. "Puss n Boots?" He laughed at his own joke. He can be pretty funny, except when he tries to be funny.

She turned her eyes on him. "Wow. You're a mind reader! How did you guess it?"

Gabe shrugged. "Just lucky. What's your real name?"

She ignored the question and turned to me. "I'm totally lost. Just wandering the halls. This school is too big for me. I can't find anything."

"Well, you found *us*," I said.

"Thank goodness." She straightened her floppy cap over her hair. "But I can't find the art room. I'm supposed to be in the art room next period. Is it on this floor?"

"No. It's on the second floor," I said. "Down the hall from the lunch room." I handed Gabe his phone. "I'll take you there," I told her.

"Oh, thank you. You're a hero. I'm totally turned around."

"Catch you later," Gabe said.

I started toward the stairs. "We have to talk about Saturday," I called back to him. "There's a big snowstorm coming. My dad says if he doesn't rent all his snowmobiles, we can take some out to the hills."

"Sweet," Gabe said. "I'll tell Diego. Kathryn, too."

The girl stayed close beside me as we climbed to the second floor. The bell was about to ring. The halls were noisy and crowded now. She sort of pressed herself against me as we walked. "This is so nice of you. I just keep getting lost here."

She smelled like flowers. Roses, maybe. I don't know flowers too well.

She flashed me an awesome smile and pressed herself against me again. She was definitely flirting with me. I mean, she wasn't too subtle. And me? Well . . . you know. Like my hands were getting sweaty. I felt almost hypnotized.

"So . . . tell me your real name," I said.

"Mary. Mary Real."

"Your real name is Real?"

She laughed. "Lizzy Walker," she said. "Seriously."

I guided her around the corner. My friend Diego waved as he hurried past. His head whipped around. I caught the surprised look on his face to see me walking with this new girl.

"Here's the art room," I said. "You can remember it. It's the room at the end of the hall with the really big windows."

Lizzy squeezed my arm. "Thanks again." She swung her backpack off her shoulders and carried it into the room.

I still felt the touch of her hand on my arm. The flowery perfume aroma lingered around me. I turned and started toward my French class downstairs in the language lab. But I'd only taken a few steps when I heard a voice behind me:

"Hey, Michael—who's your new girlfriend?"

Startled, I spun around. "Oh. Pepper. Hi."

11.

Pepper is a redhead, and redheads are supposed to be fiery and emotional and jealous. That's the stereotype. And Pepper tries to live up to that stereotype at all times. I mean, Pepper was the perfect name for her.

She has long, wavy copper-colored hair that falls to her shoulders, warm gray-green eyes, a turned-up nose (which she hates) dotted with freckles. "Face it, I'm cute," she said to me once, after we'd gotten to know one another. "And who really wants to be cute?"

"You're more than cute," I said. That's what she wanted me to say. "You look a lot like . . . uh . . . Amy Adams."

We were huddled close in my car and she pulled away from me with a jerk. "Huh? Amy Adams? But she's so *old*!"

"You know what I meant," I muttered.

I liked Pepper a lot. She was funny and fun to be with. But I did find myself *apologizing* a lot of the time I was with her.

And now, why did I feel like apologizing for walking the new girl Lizzy Walker to the art room?

I hurried over to her. She eyed me suspiciously. Like I'd just murdered her cat or something. "That's the new girl," I said. "She . . . was lost. Asked me to show her where the art room is."

"Is she crippled?" Pepper asked, twitching her nose at me. "That's why she held onto you to walk there?"

"No way. She didn't hold onto me," I said. "She squeezed my arm once. Is that what you're talking about? Listen, I wasn't coming on to her. She was lost and I was just trying to be friendly."

Pepper pushed her lips out in a pout. "Michael, I need you to be friendly to *me*." Then she wrapped her arms around my neck, pulled my face down, and pressed her lips hard against mine.

There were still a bunch of kids in the hall. Someone whistled. I tried to pull away. But Pepper tightened her armlock around my neck and kissed me some more.

And as I kissed her . . . As I kissed her . . . I couldn't help it. I found myself thinking about Lizzy.

"Hey, Scout." My friend Diego bumped up behind me after school. I was leaning into my locker, searching for a book, and the hard bump sent me crashing into the locker wall. Diego is big and wide and an all-state wrestler, and he doesn't know his own strength. Seriously. He hurts people when he's just being playful.

Gabe once called him The Enforcer, and Diego turned red and looked like he wanted to punch Gabe. He said before he was born, his grandfather was a gangster back in Mexico and got himself shot to pieces in front of his whole family. So Diego doesn't like gangster stuff.

Diego says he's nonviolent, and he'll punch out your lights if you don't think so. Ha. The guy has a good sense of humor. He's a good friend, too. And his girlfriend, Kathryn Layne, is part of our group, too. She's Pepper's best friend. She and Pepper are both going to Penn next fall.

Diego pried me from my locker and brushed off the front of my sweater with one big paw. "They're still saying snow for Saturday," he said.

"Thanks for the weather report," I said. "Do you also do sports headlines?"

He pinched my cheeks. Ouch. "Michael, you're so funny. I meant, if there's big snow, do you think your dad will let us . . ." He raised both hands like they were on handlebars and made a loud roaring sound.

I nodded. "Dad just got in some new Arctic Cats with four-stroke engines."

Diego let out a long breath. "Wow. How many horses?"

"He says one-twenty-five," I said.

Diego grinned and made that roaring sound again. Some girls at a locker across the hall giggled. I'm not sure why. One-hundred-twenty-five HP on one of these beauties is nothing to giggle about.

"We can tear up some serious snow," Diego said.

I shut the locker door and latched the combination lock. "The only problem is, the Cats might be rented by the time we get there."

Diego poked me in the shoulder. "Your pops won't save them for us?"

"You know my dad. He's not going to turn away paying customers just so we can have a party."

Diego shook his head. "Bad priorities. So who's coming on Saturday? Kathryn, right?"

"Sure," I said. "Just us. You, Kathryn, me, Pepper, and Gabe."

"A snow party. A few brews at my house before we go just to get warmed up. Then . . ." He roared again.

"Sounds like a plan," I said. We bumped knuckles. His fist is as big as a cantaloupe! He turned and lumbered away.

I picked up my backpack—and there stood Lizzy.

That troubled look on her pale face again. "I'm totally embarrassed, Michael." She grabbed my arm. "But I'm lost again. I've been lost all day. Seriously."

"I should draw you a map," I said. How could I not stare into those amazing eyes? "You know. It would have all the classrooms on it, and a red X marked *You Are Here*."

She shook her head. "I need a GPS for this school. On my phone. I'd just type in my next destination. Only they don't let you take your phone out during the day. Also . . ." I caught an instant of emotion on her face. "Also . . . I don't have a phone."

"Parents won't let you?"

She frowned. "Can't afford it."

That brought me back to the grocery store, and once again I pictured her sneaking the food into her bag. *Did I really see that?*

"I'll be the GPS," I said. I did my robot voice: "Enter a new destination, please."

She gave me a shove. "I'm just trying to find the gym. I thought I knew where it was, but I got turned around."

"That's an easy one," I said. I pointed. "Go down those steps. The gym is on the right. You'll recognize it. It says *Gym* above the door."

She laughed and shoved me again. "Thanks a lot. You know, I'm just lost, I'm not stupid."

Her hand slid down to mine. She laced her fingers with mine.

"Ouch!" I cried out as I felt a sharp pain on the tip of my pointer finger.

Startled, I stepped back from her. I saw a silvery push-pin in Lizzy's hand. I raised my finger and watched a tiny droplet of bright red blood appear on the tip.

"Hey—" I cried. "What—?"

Lizzy shoved the pin into her own finger. She pulled it out as a trickle of blood appeared on her skin. Then she raised her hand and pressed our two bleeding fingers together.

She brought her face close to mine. *"Now we're bloods,"* she whispered.

She spun away and ran down the stairs.

Listening to her footsteps, I gazed at the smear of blood on my finger.

What was THAT about?

12.

The Shadyside High yearbook is called *The Yearbook*. It's not a very clever title, but at least no one ever says, "Is this the yearbook?" Everyone knows what it is.

Pepper and I are the editors this year. We do a print edition at the end of the school year, and we write the blog online whenever we have school news and/or team news or gossip to write about.

The yearbook has a small office downstairs in the corner of the hall past the gym. I think it used to be a broom closet or maybe a phone booth because it's a really tight squeeze. Pepper and I sit on opposite ends of one desk with our laptops almost back-to-back. And there's a small table other people can use. And a file cabinet with one drawer that works.

Friday after school, I was already leaning over my laptop when Pepper came into the office. She had her coppery hair pulled back in a ponytail, which made her look about twelve. She wore the velvety dark brown vest she loves over an emerald-green T-shirt, and jeans with rips at both knees.

"Hey, Michael." She dropped her bag on the floor and slid around the desk to my side. She leaned forward to kiss me, but I moved my head, and her kiss landed on my neck.

"How's it going?" I said. "Did you survive the little surprise quiz Herman gave us?"

"Mr. Herman never counts them. So I don't sweat them." Her eyes were on my laptop screen. "Facebook?"

I nodded. "Yeah. She doesn't have a Facebook page," I said.

Pepper squinted at me. "Who? Who are you talking about?"

I blinked. "Oh. That new girl. Lizzy Walker. No Facebook page."

"Who cares?" Pepper snapped. She crossed her arms in front of her chest. "Why do you care?"

"Well . . . we're going to need yearbook info on her. Right?"

"We'll get it when we do her profile," Pepper said. "We don't need Facebook. What's your problem, Michael? Why are you fainting over that girl?"

"Huh? Me? Fainting? I wasn't fainting, Pepper. What kind of word is that, fainting? Men don't faint. Only women faint."

"Michael, it's like you're in a trance over her or something. What's so special about her?"

"Nothing," I answered quickly. "I didn't say she was special."

"Then why are you blushing?"

"I'm not blushing. It's hot in here."

Pepper leaned over me and gripped my shoulders with both hands. "Tell me the truth. There's nothing going on between you and that girl?"

I pushed her hands away. "How *could* there be? She's only been in school a couple of days. I don't know her at all."

I was desperate to change the subject. "What are we doing today?"

She still had her fists clenched, ready for a fight. I told you, she takes being a redhead very seriously. I could always tell when she was steamed about something because the freckles on her face turned darker.

"I thought we were looking through those old yearbooks," she said.

We had discovered a closet across from the library stuffed from floor to ceiling with old Shadyside yearbooks. And since this year was the hundredth anniversary of the yearbook, Pepper and I thought it would be really cool to put some old photos on the blog. And maybe publish some pages of old yearbooks with all the kids looking so weird and grown-up and wearing such dumb-looking clothes.

"Let's go check them out," I said. I clicked off Facebook,

jumped up, slid my arm around Pepper's shoulders, and we made our way to the yearbook closet.

"I sneezed twelve times," I said. "Pepper and I counted them. I thought my head was going to explode. You know. BAM! Like a balloon."

"And all the hot air would come flying out," Dad said. He laughed.

"Not funny, Mitchell," Mom scolded him.

"I get it. You think I'm an airhead," I said, dropping my fork onto the table. "Funny."

"Michael is obviously very allergic to dust," Mom continued. "Maybe he needs to see an allergy doctor." Mom is always ready to see a doctor. When I was little, she took me to a doctor because my baby teeth were a few weeks late falling out.

Dad swallowed a chunk of salmon. "Take him to a doctor because he sneezed twice? Maybe we should call 911." Dad can be very funny, especially at Mom's expense. He loves giving her a hard time. She pretty much ignores his sarcasm. She's very sweet-natured.

We were finishing our dinner. Baked salmon and linguini, my favorite because of all the melty cheese. And I was telling them about going into the yearbook closet, hoping to look at the old books. But I started sneezing so violently, I kicked up a dust storm, and Pepper had to pull me out of the closet and wait till I was sneezed out.

Dad rolled his eyes. "Next time, bring a Kleenex," he said. He forked up more linguini.

"So what did you do about the old yearbooks?" Mom asked me, passing the bowl of string beans. "Are you just going to forget the idea?"

I waved the bowl away. She knows I don't like string beans, but she never gives up.

"Pepper and I dragged a bunch of them out and took them to the yearbook office. She's going to dust them off. You know. Clean them up. And we'll try again. Most of the dust was in the closet, so—"

The front doorbell rang.

They both turned toward the living room. I jumped up. "That's Pepper," I said. "We made a plan to study together tonight for the winter midterms."

I dragged the napkin over my mouth and chin, pushed the dining room chair back, and hurried to the door.

The bell chimed again.

I pulled open the door and gasped. "Lizzy? What are *you* doing here?"

13.

Standing in the open doorway, I shivered from the sudden cold. I glimpsed a pale half moon in the night sky between curtains of clouds. Large snowflakes fell all around, caught in the yellow light from our porch light. Nearly a foot of snow already on the ground.

Lizzy wore the same floppy wool cap I'd seen in school. She had a short down parka, open in front to reveal a dark sweater pulled over her jeans. I saw her footprints in the snow, coming up the front of our yard. She wore sneakers, not boots.

"Michael, you won't believe this. But I'm lost again." She had something of a guilty smile on her face. Was it guilty, or was it playful, teasing? Her eyes were pleading with me. Pleading with me *to do what?*

I took a step onto the porch. "Lizzy . . ." A gust of wind blew droplets of wet snow into my face. "How did you know where I live?"

She shrugged in reply, that strange playful smile, almost devilish, frozen on her face.

"Is it Pepper? Why doesn't she come in?" Mom called from the dining room.

I stepped back and pushed the door open wider. "Come in. You look frozen."

Lizzy stopped on the WELCOME mat and stamped her shoes. Then she followed me into the house. *"Brrrrrrr."* She shook herself like a dog shakes when it's wet. "I've got to get some boots. My sneakers are soaked through."

The shoulders of her jacket were covered with snow, and she had a big wet patch on her back. The coat didn't appear to be waterproof. She tugged off the cap and fiddled with her black hair, pulling the sides down over her cheeks.

"Y-you're lost again?" I stammered.

She nodded. "I made a wrong turn. I—"

Mom appeared in the front hall. Her eyes went wide when she saw it wasn't Pepper. "Oh. Hello."

"Mom, this is Lizzy," I said.

Mom nodded. "Nice to meet you."

"She's new in Shadyside, and she's always getting lost," I said.

Lizzy shivered. "Sorry. I'm frozen. My teeth are chattering."

"Let's take off that wet jacket," Mom said. She stepped up and helped Lizzy out of it. "Come into the dining room and let's warm you up."

Lizzy hesitated. "Are you sure? I don't want to interrupt your dinner. I just lost my way and—"

"Come in. Come in," Mom said. She handed the jacket to me. "Go hang it in the back closet. It'll dry faster."

By the time I returned from hanging up the coat, Lizzy had already met my dad, and she had taken the place beside mine at the table. She flashed me a smile. "Your mom is so terrific. I told her I haven't eaten and—"

Mom appeared carrying a dinner plate and silverware. "I have plenty of linguini left over. And help yourself, Lizzy, to string beans." Mom brought in the big pasta bowl and began piling linguini on Lizzy's plate.

"Your family just moved here?" Dad asked, taking the last sip of his glass of red wine.

Lizzy nodded. "Last week."

"Where did you live before?" Dad asked.

"You probably never heard of it," Lizzy said. "It's a very small town. Mary's Landing?"

Dad shook his head. "Never heard of it."

Lizzy turned to her food. She began stuffing huge forkfuls of linguini into her mouth. Her chin and cheeks were soon smeared, but she didn't stop to wipe them with her napkin. She kept eating, chewing and sucking the strands of noodles down with loud gulps, as if she hadn't eaten in weeks.

Mom and dad glanced at each other, then pretended not to notice.

Mindy barked at her and stuck her snout in Lizzy's lap. Mindy likes attention from newcomers. But Lizzy was too busy eating to pet the dog.

"Where is your house? Near here?" Mom asked.

Lizzy nodded, swallowing hard. "It's on Heather Court," she said. "I thought this was Heather. But with all the snow . . ."

"This is Weaver," Dad told her. "Weaver runs right into Heather. If you'd gone one more block . . ."

"I'm totally embarrassed," Lizzy said. She squeezed my hand. "Michael must think I'm an idiot. Every time he sees me, I'm lost." She returned to the linguini, shoveling it into her mouth without taking a breath.

"Do you need to call your parents or anything?" Dad asked, watching her eat. "Will they be worried?"

She motioned no with her free hand. "Not a problem."

Dad turned to me. "I forgot to tell you, I had some cancellations for tomorrow afternoon. The Arctic Cats are rented, but I have some Yamaha Vipers for you and your friends to take out."

"Sweet!" I cried. "Thanks, Dad. That's awesome. The snow will be perfect. The guys are going to be so psyched."

Lizzy lowered her fork. Her plate was empty except for a small puddle of sauce. She pulled a short strand of linguini off her cheek. "Snowmobiles?"

"Dad owns the Snowmobile Ranch in North Hills," I told her. "A bunch of us are going to go riding along the River Road tomorrow."

"Oh, wow." She finally wiped her mouth with the napkin. Then she squeezed my hand again. "I've never been on a snowmobile. Can I come, too?"

I hesitated. "Well . . ."

"Is that a yes?" Lizzy cried.

"I guess," I said. "Okay."

"Thank you!" she cried. She leaned over and kissed me on the cheek.

And that's when I looked up and saw Pepper watching from the dining room doorway.

14.

*L*izzy pulled her face away from mine.

I saw Pepper's eyes narrow for just a second. The hood of her long down parka was still over her head. She scowled at me, then quickly made her expression a blank. "Michael? I thought we were going to study . . ."

Mom jumped to her feet. "Hi, Pepper," she said. "We didn't hear the bell."

"I didn't ring it," Pepper replied, eyes on me. "The front door was open and—"

"Open?" Dad uttered his surprise. "I *thought* it was getting cold in here."

"I'm so sorry," Lizzy said, shaking her head. "I must have left it open when I came in. I wasn't thinking straight and—and . . . I'm not having a good night." She rested her head on my shoulder.

That got a reaction from Pepper. I saw her eyes go wide for a brief second and caught the scowl again.

"Take off your coat, Pepper," Mom said. "By the way, I like that color on you. Is it violet?"

"I think it's a little darker than violet," Pepper told her. "Does it look okay with my hair? It isn't too much?"

"Not at all. I like it." Mom glanced at Lizzy, then turned back to Pepper. "Oh, I'm sorry. I'm being rude. Do you know Lizzy?"

Pepper kept her eyes locked on me. "No. No, I don't."

"Hi," Lizzy said, giving her a little wave. "Nice to meet you."

I climbed to my feet. "Pepper, the front closet is a mess. Let me help you hang up your coat." I took her by the elbow and led her back to the front hall. "I know this looks weird . . ." I whispered.

Pepper lowered her hood and head-butted me in the chest. "You told me you didn't know her," she said in an angry whisper. "Didn't you!"

"Well, yes, but—"

"You said you didn't know her. And now here she is having dinner with you, sitting next to you, and kissing you—"

"She just showed up out of the blue," I whispered, my eyes on the dining room doorway. "I didn't invite her."

"Michael, since when did you become a liar? She just showed up and sat down to dinner with your family?"

"Yes," I insisted. "No way am I lying, Pepper. Really. I—"

I stopped as Lizzy came into the room, her jacket folded

over her arm. Mom must have given it to her. "I'm going now," she said. "I'm so sorry I just burst in like that." She laughed. "One of these days, you'll see me, and I won't be lost."

"Shadyside can be confusing," Pepper said. She pointed to the front window. "The snow finally stopped, so it's easier to see where you're going."

Lizzy fixed the cap over her hair. "Nice to meet you, Pepper."

"Nice to meet you," Pepper echoed without enthusiasm.

Lizzy brushed past me. "See you tomorrow."

"Tomorrow?" Pepper raised her eyes to me.

"Where should I meet you?" Lizzy asked.

"Why don't you meet us at my dad's store," I said. "It's on the River Road. You really can't miss it." I laughed. "Even *you* can't miss it. It's nearly a block long."

Pepper couldn't keep the surprise from her voice. "You're coming with us tomorrow afternoon?"

Lizzy nodded. She gave Pepper a strange smile. "Michael invited me."

That wasn't exactly true. Lizzy had invited herself. But before I had a chance to say anything, Lizzy was out the door.

A blast of cold air invaded the room. Pepper's stare was even colder. I pushed the front door closed.

"Lighten up," I said. "She's new in town and she doesn't know anybody. What's the harm in being nice to her?"

Pepper nodded and took my arm. "You're right. You're

totally right. What's the harm? Just because she's drop-dead gorgeous . . ."

My mouth dropped open. "Excuse me? You think she's so gorgeous?"

Pepper gave me a shove. "Seriously, Michael. Don't pretend you didn't notice." She hoisted up her backpack, and we started toward my room to study. But I stopped at the front window. The streetlamp at the bottom of the driveway lit up the sidewalk. "Hey, look," I said.

Pepper leaned close to the window and followed my gaze.

"It's Lizzy," I said. "She's going in the wrong direction. She's not heading toward Heather Court. She's walking the wrong way."

15.

Saturday started out beautiful. The sky was an amazing blue. Not a cloud to be seen. The sun floated low in the sky and made the snow sparkle like gold. The air felt cold and fresh and made my whole face tingle. One of those perfect winter days where the whole world is quiet, as if under a blanket, and nothing can go wrong.

We started out at Diego's house an hour or so after lunch. Diego's parents were away, and they don't care if he drinks beer, anyway. So we sprawled on the floor in his den and played *Madden Football* on his PlayStation and had a few cans of Miller Lite. Just to warm up and get the whole snowmobile party off to a good start.

Kathryn told a story about running into Miss Curdy at the gym and how totally embarrassing it was to be working out with your English teacher there. Kathryn is Diego's girlfriend. She is about half Diego's size. Seriously. Her head comes up to his chest.

She has white-blonde hair cut very short, blonde eye-brows, and huge pale blue eyes, and the greatest laugh, from deep in her throat. She is a riot. She can tell a stupid story about running into a teacher at the gym and have us all rolling on the floor.

Diego jumped to his feet and did a victory dance, pumping his fists above his head. His team had just scored a touchdown. Gabe smashed an empty beer can on his fore-head. Just because he's Gabe and he doesn't want anyone to think he's too mature.

"When are we going?" Pepper demanded, standing up to pass a large bag of popcorn to Diego. Pepper, impatient as always. "Are we waiting for the snow to melt?"

"Anyone want another beer?" Gabe had his priorities and Pepper had hers.

I glanced out the window. The wind was blowing the snow around in Diego's backyard. It was still very pow-dery. I emptied my beer can and tossed it into the trash can in the corner. "Okay, let's roll."

It was a short ride to my dad's Snowmobile Ranch. There were a few slick spots on the streets, but they'd mostly been plowed. I drove carefully, keeping both hands tightly on the wheel and watching my speed. I didn't want to be stopped by any cops. They'd smell the beer on my breath, and that could be trouble.

Pepper sat beside me. I was driving my mom's Corolla, and Diego took up half the back seat. Kathryn had to scrunch her head down and sit on his lap, which he didn't mind at all. Gabe was squeezed beside Diego. "I . . . I can't breathe. . . ." he choked out. We didn't pay any attention to him.

I pulled into the store's gravel parking lot. Sure enough, Lizzy was there waiting for us at the back of the building. She waved a red-gloved hand as I parked by the back entrance.

I turned to see Pepper's reaction. "Don't worry. I'm going to be nice to her," Pepper said. "You were right, Michael. She's new and she doesn't have any friends and . . . there's something kind of sad about her."

I nodded, happy and a little relieved to hear Pepper's decision. She can be jealous and impatient and fiery-tempered— but she's also a sweetheart when she wants to be.

I climbed out of the car and pulled the back door open. "Diego, do I have to get the Jaws of Life to pull you out of there?"

He laughed. I took Kathryn's arm and tugged her out first. Diego rolled out with a loud groan. Gabe was already standing on the other side of the car, taking deep breaths.

Lizzy came trotting over. She had a red wool ski cap to match her red wool gloves. She wore a blue down parka and furry brown Ugg boots that looked brand-new.

"I'm so excited!" she gushed. "I've never been on a snow-mobile before. How do you drive it, Michael? Is it kind of like a bike?"

"Not much like a bike," I said.

"You don't have to pedal it," Diego added helpfully.

"My dad will give you a complete tutorial," I said.

"It's not very hard," Gabe said. "Even Diego can drive one."

Diego gave Gabe a hard shove that sent him barreling into the side of the car. "You're so not funny."

"Don't play rough," Gabe said. "I'll tell my mommy."

Kathryn held her stomach. "I shouldn't have had those two beers. I forgot I didn't eat lunch." She groaned.

"You'll forget about it when we're blasting across River Ridge," Diego said. "But if you feel sick, you can just lean to one side and vomit in the snow."

Kathryn took Diego's arm. "You're so sensitive."

Dad had everything ready to go. The Snow Cats were all rented out, as he had said. But the Yamahas were looking awesome. He showed Lizzy how to sit on one, where to put her feet, and how to work the few controls. "Don't go too fast," he told me. "Give her a chance to get the feel of it."

"No problem," I said.

Dad's store is at the bottom of the River Road. It's a great location. Wide paths start at the back of the store and cut along the side of the road, perfect for snowmobiling.

The road follows the Conononka River, then climbs the hills up to River Ridge, the highest point in Shadyside. There are thick woods up there. No houses. It's protected park land. You can stand on the highest cliff and look down on the curving river and the town far below.

And what a *rush* to roar along the wide clearing up

there with the river cliffs on one side and the dark woods on the other, kicking up high waves of snow, scooting and sliding and shooting through the snow banks, feeling like you're lost in a cold, shimmering white world of your own.

Ha. Very poetic, right? Well, I told you I want to study creative writing.

We took off, the six of us. The path wasn't wide enough to go side by side. Diego and Kathryn led the way. The two of them are pros. Gabe and Pepper came exploding right behind them, kicking up a snowstorm on all sides of them. I stayed in back, riding beside Lizzy. We took our time. Her steering was unsteady. She kept slowing down, then speeding up again.

"Slide!" I shouted. "Give it some gas, then stop. Don't be afraid to slide."

She nodded, but her dark eyes were wide, her face tight with concentration. The others were pulling ahead. They made the first turn, following the path as it climbed the hills.

I knew it wouldn't take her long to get control of the thing. I remembered my first try. I'd felt as if I was sitting on top of a wild animal, or maybe an untrained bucking bronco. The animal was roaring, in total control, and I was along for the ride, helpless . . . totally helpless.

Lizzy had that same look of panic on her face. But after a few minutes, I could see the tension fade. She actually smiled as her ride smoothed out, and we sailed together over the powdery snow banks.

Soon, we were high above the river. I glanced down and saw the shiny white ice stretched over the water. The river was nearly frozen from bank to bank.

We were close to the top, almost to River Ridge. And the path opened into a wide, flat clearing. Pine trees lined the horizon to our left, the start of the miles of tangled woods.

Diego and Kathryn spun their snowmobiles in a wide circle. They slid wildly, spinning, kicking up a wall of white powder. Gabe and Pepper joined the fun. They spun and slid as if they were riding on an icy pond.

The thunder of our engines rang off the trees. We shouted and pumped our fists in the air and sent tsunamis of snow rolling high in the sky, and the waves of silvery flakes came down over all of us like a frozen shower.

Lizzy hung back. I motioned to her to try spinning out. But maybe that was too much for the first time. She moved slowly in a wide circle, watching the rest of us go crazy.

I came out of a fast spin and motioned to Lizzy to follow me. I straightened up, got control, and began racing toward the fresh snow along the tree line.

What was that red bird soaring so low overhead? Was it a hawk?

When I lowered my gaze, I caught Lizzy moving in a straight line toward me. Then I turned—and gasped as I saw someone come walking out of the trees.

I squinted against the blowing snow until he came into focus. A guy about my age, maybe a little older, in a long black overcoat, a dark hood over his head with black hair spilling out, down to his shoulders.

He took long strides, moving away from the trees. It took me a few seconds to realize my snowmobile was rocketing right toward him. A straight collision path. Why didn't he see me? Why didn't he hear the grind and the roar?

I grabbed the control and tried to turn.

"Hey—!" I cried out. Something was wrong. Something was very wrong with me. I suddenly couldn't move. My arms hung helplessly. I tried . . . tried . . . But I couldn't swerve or spin away.

I tried again. My hands slid off the control. My arms dropped to my sides. I felt too weak to hold them up.

What is happening to me?

I tried to jam the brake. My boot suddenly felt as if it weighed a thousand pounds. My leg refused to move. My foot went limp. I . . . I couldn't stop the thing. And I couldn't turn. I couldn't swerve. Struggling, straining, I couldn't move my arms or legs!

The guy walked with his head down. His arms swung gently at his sides in the big overcoat. He didn't hear me. He didn't see me.

I stared helplessly as my snowmobile rammed into him with a ferocious *thud*. Caught him in the side. Knocked him back hard. I watched his body leave the ground. The impact of the crash lifted him high in the air.

I saw his eyes go wild, and I heard his scream. A scream

I knew I'd hear for the rest of my life. A scream of pain and horror.

My snowmobile darted past him. Suddenly, I could move again. My arms came back to life. I clenched and unclenched my fingers. Working. My legs were working, too.

No time to think about what had paralyzed me. I killed the engine and slid to a stop in a tall snowdrift. I sat there breathing hard for a few seconds, my head spinning, shaking in disbelief.

Then I stood up, struggling to shake off the dizziness, I turned. I saw the young man flat on his back in the snow, one leg tilted at an odd angle. His hood had come off and his long black hair was spread on the snow around his head.

Lizzy was already down on her knees at his side. She bent over him, one hand on the young man's chest. Lizzy turned when she saw me running toward her. Her eyes were wide with alarm.

"He's dead, Michael!" she screamed. "You killed him!"

16.

Her shrill cries rang in my ears. My head throbbed. I pressed my hands against my ears, trying to shut out her words.

"He's dead, Michael. You killed him!"

A long moan escaped my throat. The others pulled into a line facing us. They remained on their snowmobiles as if frightened to climb off.

Pepper hugged herself. I could see her whole body shuddering. Diego hunched forward, his expression grim. Kathryn and Gabe shielded their eyes to squint into the snow.

"Michael, you plowed right into him. Didn't you see him?" Gabe asked.

"Why didn't he see *me*?" I answered. I didn't want to tell them how my arms and legs froze. I didn't understand it. I'd never panicked like that before. "I . . . couldn't stop," I added. "I tried, but . . ."

"We have to get out of here," Diego said, glancing all around. "Before someone comes."

"Are you *crazy*?" Pepper cried. "Just leave him here?"

"He's dead. There's nothing we can do for him," Diego said. "Look. We can't hang around. We had some beers, right? The police will bust us."

"But it was an accident," I said.

"They won't care," Diego insisted. "They'll do a breath test or something and find out we were drinking."

"A total accident—" I repeated, still feeling dazed and dizzy. The snow glared in my eyes. Nothing seemed real.

"Diego is right," Gabe said. "We'll be arrested. They'll say we were drunk. Drunk high school kids out for a thrill ride and we killed a guy. Forget our college scholarships. They'll be out the window. Our lives will be ruined."

"But we can't leave him," Pepper argued. "Is he really dead? Lizzy, is he breathing? There's just a trickle of blood from his head. Maybe . . ."

"Let's go! Let's beat it!" Diego cried, making his engine roar.

"No. Wait—!" Pepper insisted. "Wait. Everybody, calm down. We have to think clearly."

"I'm thinking clearly about our future," Gabe said. "Why ruin our lives forever? The guy is dead. We can't help him. We have to save ourselves."

Suddenly, Lizzy chimed in. She was still on her knees in the snow, leaning over the young man's body. "I . . . I think I know him," she said. She brushed a strand of his black hair off his forehead. His eyes stared blankly up at the sky.

A shadow swept over the snow. I gazed up to see that same red hawk swooping low. It turned in midair and floated into the line of pine trees.

A hush fell over the scene. We all froze and waited for Lizzy to continue.

"Oh, wow. Yes. I know him," Lizzy said. "His name is Angel. He . . . he was at my old school for a while. . . ." Her voice trailed off. She suddenly turned away from him and raised her gaze to me.

"He was at my old school, Michael, but he got in trouble. Major trouble."

I swallowed. "Major trouble like . . . ?"

"He beat two kids. Almost to death. Everyone knew it was Angel who did it. But somehow, he got off with a warning."

"Whoa," Diego muttered. "A bad dude."

"He's a total psychopath," Lizzy said. "Seriously. Everyone was terrified of him. He was the angriest person I ever saw. He picked up a teacher in the lunchroom and shoved his head through a glass door. The teacher never came back to school."

"Let's go," Diego said, roaring his engine again. "We've got to get away from here."

"He's right." Lizzy jumped to her feet and wiped the knees of her jeans off with both hands. She climbed onto her snowmobile. "The guy is bad news. Let's go. Hurry."

This time, no one argued. We turned our snowmobiles and headed back down from River Ridge. No one looked back.

I killed someone. The thought repeated in my mind.

I pictured the startled look on Angel's face as my snowmobile rammed into his side. And I saw his body fly into the air, arms and legs thrashing crazily. How could I make the images stop repeating?

As I saw the accident again and again, I kept remembering the feeling of being paralyzed. My arms and legs weak and helpless. Frozen. I was frozen in panic. How else to explain it?

We were roaring downhill, following the wide path beside the River Road. Lizzy and I led the way, followed by Diego and Kathryn. Gabe and Pepper had fallen behind.

The sun was still high in the sky. We sent up tall waves of snow as we sped downhill, taking the curves easily as the road wound down to the bottom.

Suddenly, I raised a hand. I skidded to a stop. "Wait!" I shouted over the roar of their engines. I turned and watched them slide as they braked their snowmobiles. We were all at jagged angles. It looked like a car accident on the highway when a bunch of cars plow into each other.

Accident. All an accident. The words tumbled through my mind.

"Michael, what's wrong?" Gabe shouted. "Why'd you stop?"

"We have to go back," I said. "We're being stupid."

They all started talking at once. I raised my hand again until they stopped. "We've made a terrible mistake," I shouted. My voice rang down the hill. "What if he's still alive? I don't care if he's a bad dude or not. We can't leave him to die in the snow. Then it wouldn't be an accident. It would be murder."

"It's too late, Michael," Diego argued. "We can't—"

"We can't leave the scene of the accident," I told him. "We weren't thinking clearly. Do you think the police won't see our snowmobile tracks? Of course they will. And it won't take them long to track down who made them."

"Michael is right," Pepper said. "Six snowmobiles from his dad's store? They'll find us in less than an hour. And we'll be in even more trouble because we left the guy lying there."

"Let's turn around and go back," I said. "We'll call the police. We'll tell them how it was an accident. Everyone agreed?"

No one protested.

Lizzy caught my eye. She had her head down, as if she was thinking hard. Then she raised her gaze to me. Her dark eyes studied me. She nodded. She agreed with me. I had this strange feeling. Like she and I were connecting, like we were suddenly close.

We slid our snowmobiles around and began climbing the hill again. Now the wind was in our faces, freezing gusts that made my cheeks hurt. I pulled my ski cap lower, but it didn't protect my face.

It seemed to take an hour to climb back up to River Ridge. The heavy feeling of dread in my stomach felt colder than the swirling wind.

I reached the spot by the tree line first. I stopped. And blinked. And squinted hard.

"Where is he?" Lizzy cried. The others murmured their disbelief.

He was gone. I could see the indentation in the snow. See where his head had been. His back. His leg, bent at such an odd angle. I saw a thin line of pink, left from where his head was bleeding.

But no body. No body sprawled in the snow.

"At least we know he's alive," I managed to say.

"But he's a psychopath, Michael," Lizzy said in a tiny voice. "And he knows who we are. He knows who we are. We . . . we could be in a lot of trouble."

PART TWO

SHADYSIDE, 1950

17.

Gina Palmieri was relieved to see the two policemen at her door. She had been waiting for news for five days and unable to do anything else. The house hadn't been cleaned. The dishes were piled still dirty in the sink. She hadn't even made the bed.

She hadn't slept, either. How could she sleep without Angelo in the house? With Beth gone, too. With no word about either of them.

The cousins had come over to keep her company, but she couldn't talk to them. Was she supposed to make small talk? Did they expect her to feed them?

She couldn't eat. Her stomach was a tight knot. And now she sat with a cup of tea growing cold on the table beside her, an unopened magazine folded between her hands.

And at last through the front window, she could see the two dark-uniformed officers come up the front walk. She was at the door before they rang the bell.

And as they removed their caps, she could read their faces and knew the news was bad.

How could it be good?

Angelo and Beth didn't go off on a vacation together. They weren't out celebrating the opening of the stables without her.

Something terrible had happened to them. Mrs. Palmieri led the two solemn-faced officers into the front room and motioned for them to sit on the low brown couch. She stood behind the matching armchair, hands gripping the back as if it were a life raft.

"Mrs. Palmieri, perhaps you could sit down," the officer who had introduced himself as Sergeant O'Brian said, gesturing.

She shook her head. Her dark eyes avoided his stare. "I'm okay here."

O'Brian nodded. His partner, Officer Mannelli, shifted his weight uncomfortably. It was an old couch, Gina knew, and no one was ever comfortable on it. But this was different.

"Have you found my husband?" Her voice came out in a croak. She hadn't spoken to anyone all morning. "My daughter Beth?"

The officers exchanged glances. "We have bad news," O'Brian said. He twirled his cap between his hands. "Your husband is dead, Mrs. Palmieri."

Gina was expecting it, but she gasped anyway. She knew she'd remember the officer's voice and the way he said the word *dead*. She knew it would become a memory she couldn't erase.

O'Brian leaned forward over the coffee table. "We found your husband's body in the Fear Street Woods."

Gina felt her knees start to give way. She moved around the chair and dropped into it. Her heart throbbed in her chest. She thought she might die. Join Angelo. It would be so much easier to die now.

"In the woods? What was he doing in the woods?" The words came out of her mouth without her thinking them. It was like she was in a dream, a very real dream, but she was outside her body watching herself, watching herself sit in her living room and talk about Angelo being dead in the woods.

"We don't know, ma'am," Mannelli said. "Our investigation has just started and—"

"Can I see him?" Her voice still a hoarse croak.

"I don't think that would be wise," Mannelli said.

"Some animals must have gotten to him," O'Brian said. "Wolves, maybe. His body . . . it's . . . uh . . . there . . . there isn't much left of him."

A sob escaped Gina's throat. *I'm not going to cry,* she told herself. *I'm not going to cry until they leave. Then I'll cry for you, Angelo. I'll cry for us both. For a long long time.*

"I know this is a horrible shock," O'Brian said softly. "But we're looking at murder here. Your husband was tied up and dragged into the woods. Before the animals got to him."

Gina sighed, her throat tight, every muscle in her body clenched.

"I'm sure you don't want to talk now," O'Brian said softly. "But do you have any idea who . . . ?" His voice trailed off.

Gina squeezed the arms of the chair until her hands ached. "What about my daughter?" she asked, ignoring O'Brian's question. "Where is she? What happened to Beth?"

"We don't know," O'Brian replied in a voice just above a whisper. "Perhaps she ran away to escape the murderer. Perhaps your husband's murderer, grabbed her, kidnapped her, took her away with him."

Gina narrowed her eyes at O'Brian. "Ran away? If Beth ran away, she'd call me from wherever she is. She wouldn't go five days without calling me. And why do you say kidnapped? I . . . I haven't received a call for ransom."

A sob escaped her throat. "My baby isn't coming home. My baby is dead."

O'Brian sighed. "There's always hope, Mrs. Palmieri."

Hope? She thought. *Look at his face. I don't see any hope there.*

"We've been searching the woods for your daughter for these five days," Mannelli said, tensely curling and uncurling his fists. "No trace of her. I'm afraid we have to call off our search."

"So you *do* think she's dead," Gina persisted.

Both men shrugged. Their uniform shirts looked heavy, uncomfortable. Both of their faces were bathed in sweat.

"Martin Dooley killed my husband," Gina said suddenly, in a flat, dry, emotionless voice. She said the words with a clenched jaw.

The two officers had started to climb up from the couch. But they sat back down upon hearing these words. "What did you say?" Mannelli asked.

"You heard me," she said in a whisper. "Martin Dooley murdered my husband and probably my daughter, too."

"Why do you say that?" Manelli asked.

"I told the other officers five days ago," Gina said angrily. "Don't you talk to each other? I . . . don't understand why no one listens to me, why no one takes me seriously."

O'Brian scratched his short white crewcut. The white hair, the tired eyes, and the deep creases on his ruddy cheeks revealed that he'd been a cop for a long time. "You reported that Martin Dooley threatened your husband."

Gina nodded. "He wasn't subtle about it, Officer. He said he would stop Angelo from running his own stable. He said he would make sure Angelo's stable failed within a year."

"But Dooley didn't threaten your husband with violence?" O'Brian asked.

"It . . . it turned into a shouting match," Gina said. "I'm afraid Angelo lost his temper. He hit Martin Dooley, nearly knocked him down."

"And then Dooley threatened to kill him?" Mannelli asked.

Gina shook her head. "He said he would pay him back. And he did, Officer. He did. And he didn't wait long. He killed my husband and my daughter, and I don't understand why you two are sitting here talking to me when he is still walking around completely free."

Mannelli started to reply, but O'Brian motioned for him to stop. "We talked to Martin Dooley several times, Mrs. Palmieri," O'Brian said, locking his eyes on hers. "We haven't been sitting around."

"Martin Dooley has an alibi," Mannelli said. "He was home with his family and two of his neighbors that whole night. He never went out."

"He's lying!" Gina jumped to her feet. "He's a filthy liar!"

"His family swears to it, and so do the neighbors," O'Brian said. "They had a small dinner party. They listened to Bob Hope on the radio. Then they played cards till after eleven. We collected all their stories separately, and they all agree. Martin Dooley could not have killed your husband and daughter."

Gina clenched her cold hands into tight fists. "You're wrong. I know he did. I know he killed them." She stood over the two policemen, shaking her fists in front of them. "What do I have to do? Prove it myself?"

18.

The chapel was decked with flowers, long colorful bouquets across the altar, wreaths resting against the sides of the two pinewood coffins, a smaller wreath on the priest's podium.

Gina had sworn she would not cry at the funeral. But the strong aroma of the lilies made her eyes water. She pulled down the black veil from her hat. She didn't want people to watch her face.

The gray, sunless morning of sleet and freezing rain was perfect for the occasion, she thought. No matter how many flowers are around me, *I'm going to live in this gray cold world from now on.*

The idea of the double funeral wasn't just an economical idea. She knew Beth was dead. Why prolong the heartache? Also, Beth would want to be beside her father. *The two of them were so close,* she remembered. *They didn't have the stormy soap-opera relationship Beth had with me.*

Although . . . Beth knew I loved her. She always knew that.

A shiny-faced usher helped Aunt Hannah down the chapel aisle. She moved so slowly and carefully these days with a cane in each hand.

Hannah made her way to the front row, took Gina's gloved hands in hers, and squeezed them tightly. The two women didn't say a word. What more was there to say? They had talked two or three times a day since the night of the murders.

Hannah held onto Gina's hands for a long moment. Then she turned and moved to sit next to cousins David and Mariana in the second row. Their son Peter was having trouble sitting still, as usual, and he kept tugging and fiddling with the black-and-white striped necktie his parents made him wear.

"Why can't I see Uncle Angelo?" he demanded.

The question made Gina cringe, but she didn't turn around to face Peter. She bit her lip hard to keep from crying. How awful that poor, innocent Peter had to face death at such an early age. How confused—and frightened—he must be.

"You have to be quiet in church, remember?" Mariana told him.

"Why can't I see Uncle Angelo?" the four-year-old repeated, this time in a loud whisper.

Gina turned in her seat. "Don't worry," she told Peter. "Uncle Angelo is watching you. From heaven."

Peter stared back at her, thinking hard. She knew that

would confuse him. But maybe it would make him stop asking that question.

Before turning back to the front, Gina glanced at the crowd. The chapel was nearly filled. Angelo had a lot of friends. A lot of cousins and a lot of friends. The sad, silent faces were a testimony to how much they liked and admired him.

But, wait.

Gina squinted through the veil. Her vision must be distorted by the black lace. She must be seeing things.

Her heart felt as if it jumped to her throat. She tossed back the veil as she jumped to her feet. And stared in shock at Martin Dooley.

Martin Dooley, in a black suit, his hat between his hands. Martin Dooley seated on the aisle near the back of the chapel, chatting nonchalantly with a man Gina didn't recognize.

A hoarse cry escaped Gina's throat. Without even realizing it, she was running now, pushing people out of the way, stumbling, charging up the aisle, screaming, screaming words she couldn't even hear because of the roar of fury in her ears.

She flew up to Martin Dooley, snatched the fedora from his hands, struggled to rip it, to tear it in half. "How dare you? How *dare* you come to his funeral?" she shrieked.

A hush fell over the chapel. People turned to watch. The organ player stopped the music abruptly. Father McCann poked his head in from the vestibule.

Gina tossed the hat at Martin Dooley's face. "How *dare* you show up here?" She pressed her trembling hands against the waist of her black skirt, her chest heaving up and down.

Dooley didn't move. He gazed up at her calmly. The only sign of tension on his face were the two blotches of red that formed on his well-shaved cheeks. "I came to pay my respects," he said softly.

"Pay your respects? You *murderer!*" Gina shrieked. She lunged at him. But two ushers appeared, grabbed her arms, held her back.

"I came to pay my respects," Dooley repeated, still not making any attempt to stand up. "You misjudge me, Mrs. Palmieri. Angelo worked for my family since he was a boy. I truly thought of him as a son."

"LIAR!" Gina screamed. "LIAR!" She struggled to free herself from the young ushers' grasp, but the two boys held tight.

"Did you forget?" Dooley continued. "I lost my nephew that same night. Aaron vanished without a trace."

Gina leaned over him, breathing hard. If only she could kill him with her stare. Send a bolt of lightning into his head, blow up that smug face.

"I lost Aaron that night, remember?" Dooley repeated. "I know your daughter Beth had something to do with it. Everyone knew your daughter was a *witch!*"

Pain stabbed Gina's temples, and she grabbed the sides of her head, as if trying to shut out that word. Something snapped. She could feel herself burn, beyond anger, beyond anything she had ever felt before.

With a furious scream, she spun her body hard, sending the two frightened ushers tumbling backward.

"MURDERER! MURDERER!"

She staggered back a few rows. Grabbed a lighted candle from its holder in the aisle. Lurched forward—and *stabbed* it into Dooley's left eye.

His hoarse scream rang off the chapel rafters as he leaped to his feet. Screams rang out all around.

He staggered into the aisle, the burning candle plunged deep in his eye socket. His hands flailed helplessly at his sides, as if he was too terrified to think, too terrified to grab the candle and pull it out.

Gina stepped back and watched as Dooley's face appeared to flame. And then, with a dry *whoosh,* his hair caught fire.

"*Do* something!" a woman behind her screamed. "Somebody—do something!"

Gina crossed her arms in front of her chest and watched.

PART
THREE

PRESENT DAY

19.

What did I just step in?"

Gabe laughed. "It's only mud, Michael. The ground is so muddy here, we could sink right into the graves."

"Cool," I said.

Diego tilted his head to one side, stuck his hands straight out in front of him, and staggered stiff-legged down the row of graves. "It's the zombie apocalypse," he growled. "I need to eat flesh." He bit the sleeve of Gabe's parka.

Gabe growled back at him, snapping his teeth. "I see dead people!" he cried. "All around. Dead people. Look. I'm stepping on them." He stomped around in a circle, his shoes sinking into the soft mud.

I shook my head. "Can't take you anywhere. You guys act as if you've never been in a graveyard before."

"Have you three found your graves yet?" Miss Beach called. She stood looking down on our class from a gently sloping hill covered in rows of tilted, gray tombstones.

"Not yet," I shouted back. "We're still looking."

Just like Miss Beach to take us to the old graveyard on the coldest, grayest, foggiest, eeriest day of the winter. Kind of perfect, I guess, for making gravestone rubbings.

Pepper motioned to me from down a long row of graves. A strong gust of wind sent her jacket flapping behind her. "Over here, Michael. Kathryn and I found some of the oldest ones. They're from like 1790."

"Too old," I said, shaking my head. "They'll be rubbed smooth."

"Since when are you the expert?" she yelled.

"I used to be a grave robber," I said. "I collected skulls when I was in first grade. My mom made me stop. She said they were unsanitary."

"You're sick," she shouted.

I laughed. "You don't believe me?"

She made a face and turned back to Kathryn and the little square gravestones they'd found.

"Hey, guys, stop wasting time," Miss Beach called. The wind blew her hood back and her blonde hair flew about her face.

"She's totally hot," Diego said.

Gabe laughed. "Seriously?"

Diego shrugged. "Just saying."

Gabe was squatting in front of a tall tombstone. It had two angels engraved at the top and fancy decorations all down the sides. I stepped up behind him and read the name cut deep in the stone: COLONEL FREDERICH DEVERAUX. Beneath the name, I could make out the words *A Leader A Gentleman A Soldier*.

Diego bumped me out of the way. "This is awesome. Miss Beach will go nuts over this one."

Gabe stood up and slid a sheet of rubbing paper from his bag. "Okay. We'll do this one. Help me hold it down, Michael. The wind is crazy."

Gabe and I pressed the paper against the front of the stone. Diego began rubbing with a stick of charcoal. We had almost finished the rubbing when Gabe turned to me, a troubled expression on his face.

"What's wrong?" I asked. The wind made the top of the paper flap as if it was trying to fly away.

"Doesn't being here creep you out?" Gabe said. I could see he wasn't joking.

"Hey, let me finish," Diego said, bending over Gabe to reach the bottom of the stone.

Gabe hesitated. "I mean, I keep thinking about that guy you hit. You know. Angel. How did he just vanish like that?"

"He got up and walked away," Diego said. "Enough about that. Shut up."

"But . . . Lizzy said he was dead," Gabe replied. "She checked him, remember? She said he was dead."

"So now you think Lizzy is a doctor?" Diego said, jabbing Gabe in the side with the charcoal. "You think she's a medical expert? She pronounced him dead so he has to be dead?"

"But I *saw* him," Gabe replied. "He *was* dead. Definitely."

I turned and saw Miss Beach watching us from the hill. "Guys," I said, "we can't talk about this now. Seriously. The wind carries our voices. We don't want . . ."

I stopped when I saw Lizzy on a low rise near the cemetery fence. She stood all alone in front of two slender tombstones, a sheet of paper flapping in her hand, her back to everyone.

I walked over to her, my shoes squishing in the mud. Wisps of fog hovered low over the ground, and beyond them a wall of thick fog was floating closer. "Hey," I called.

She was concentrating so hard on the tombstones, she didn't hear me. I stepped up behind her and touched the shoulder of her down coat, and she jumped.

She turned, blinking hard. "Oh, hi, Michael."

"What did you find?" I asked. "Something good?"

Her dark eyes studied me for a moment, and I thought I detected a tremble of sadness on her face. She pointed. "Look at these stones."

I stepped up next to her and leaned down to read the first granite stone. The engraving had been worn down by the years of weather, but the inscription was easy to read: ANGELO PALMIERI. 1912–1950. Then I turned and squinted at the second stone: BETH PALMIERI. 1934–1950.

"Side by side," Lizzy murmured. "And they both died the same year."

"A man and wife?" I said.

Lizzy's dark hair fluttered in a gust of wind. She didn't move to tug it back down, just let it fly around her face. "No. She must have been his daughter," she said. "Look at the dates."

Yes. Beth Palmieri would have been sixteen when she died.

"So sad," Lizzy said. She suddenly pressed her cheek against mine. "Oh, wow. You're as cold as I am."

I realized I wanted her to keep her cheek there, to stay so close to me. I started to slide my arm around her waist.

But she turned quickly and raised the large sheet of paper in her hand. "Help me do this rubbing. Then maybe Miss Beach will come to her senses and let us go back to the warm school."

I took the sheet of paper and spread it across the front of Angelo Palmieri's stone. I could still feel Lizzy's cheek against mine. Lizzy dug in her bag and pulled out a stick of charcoal.

She moved to begin the rubbing, but I stood up. I thought I saw something. Something moving in the patch of gravestones across from us.

The fog swirled in the wind, light at the top, then thick and gray near the ground, like a living thing, like an enormous creature oozing over the mud. I squinted hard. It was like peering through a dark window curtain.

"Michael? What is it?" Lizzy's voice suddenly seemed far away.

I stared hard and saw the man. Yes. A man rising up in the billowing fog. He was a blur of black against the gray wall of fog, but I could see him clearly. I could see him climbing up from a grave.

20.

Hey—!" I shouted.

I recognized him. I recognized the black overcoat, his long black hair, blowing around his face. Angel. Yes. Definitely the guy Lizzy called Angel. Shrouded in fog, floating out from behind a tall monument.

He stood there staring back at me, motionless as the gravestones all around. Stood there, watching. Threatening?

"Lizzy, do you see him?" I cried.

I didn't wait for her reply. I took off, running toward him, the clouds of gray thick around my legs, my heart suddenly pounding. I didn't think. I didn't hesitate. Just took off running to him, shouting, "Hey! Hey, you!" my shoes plopping noisily in the mud.

And when I reached the monument, a tall rectangular stone, shiny like marble, with a large cross on the top . . . when I reached the monument, breathing hard, squinting into the thick mist . . . he was gone.

I grabbed the monument with both gloved hands and

held on, struggling to catch my breath. Leaned against the cold marble and peered all around, watching for any movement, any sign of him. But no. He had vanished.

Back to the grave?

Back to the grave I had seen him climb out of?

Finally, I let go of the monument. I started to turn back to the others—and someone grabbed my shoulder.

I let out a cry. Spun around. "Lizzy."

Her eyes burned into mine. She wrapped me in a hug. "Michael, you looked so frightened. What did you see? What *was* it?"

"I'm not sure," I said, holding her close.

Diego stomped across our kitchen and pulled open the fridge door. He leaned into the light, examining each shelf. Then he turned back to me. "No beer?"

I shook my head. "Diego, you know my parents don't have beer in the house."

He pulled out a Coke and shut the fridge door. "Why not? They're alcoholics?"

"No," I said. "They're afraid *you* might come over and drink it all."

Gabe and Kathryn, sitting across from me at the kitchen table, burst out laughing. Pepper sat at the end of the table with her arms crossed in front of her yellow sweater. She had arrived at my house in a bad mood but didn't seem interested in talking about it. Lizzy was perched at the counter across from the table, dipping into a big bag of tortilla chips. Diego dropped down on the tall stool next to her and began pawing up chips with both hands.

"Did you all have dinner?" I asked. "There's some left-over ham if anyone wants a sandwich."

"Michael, you're such a good host," Pepper muttered.

"Where are your parents?" Diego asked with a mouth-ful of chips. "Out drinking beer?"

"You are so not funny tonight," Kathryn said.

"Huh? You kidding? I'm a riot," Diego replied.

"They're visiting my cousins in Martinsville," I said. "They wanted me to come, but I told them I had too much homework."

"You lied to your parents," Gabe said.

"Like *you* always tell the truth?" I said. "What should I have told them, Gabe? That I killed a guy on the snow-mobile on Saturday, and today he rose up from a grave in the cemetery, and I thought we should all get together tonight and talk about what to do about him?"

"They wouldn't believe that, anyway," Gabe said. "Better to lie."

"So what *are* we going to do?" Pepper said impatiently. She swept both hands back through her coppery hair.

"If he's a zombie, we have to kill him again," Diego said. He laughed at his own joke.

"I don't think he's a zombie—" I started.

"But you said you saw him climb up from a grave," Gabe said.

"It was so foggy," I replied. "I'm not sure what I saw. I

only know I recognized him. It was Angel, and he was staring at me, just standing there staring at me."

"He was dead," Lizzy chimed in. She dropped down from the tall stool and walked over to us at the table. "I know he was dead."

"But, Lizzy, if he walked away . . ." Kathryn said.

"He couldn't be alive," Lizzy insisted. "I examined him. I couldn't be mistaken. He wasn't breathing. His eyes were dead. They were like glass. Like doll's eyes. And he wasn't breathing."

"Then . . . what are you saying?" Pepper said. "That Michael saw Angel's ghost this morning?"

"His spirit," Lizzy replied. "It must be his spirit. Maybe his spirit lives on in that graveyard."

No one said anything for a long moment. I think we were all studying Lizzy to see if she was being serious.

She was.

Diego snickered. "You believe in spirits?" he asked.

"Of course," Lizzy said. "We all have spirits. We all have souls. Don't you think our souls can live on outside our bodies? Don't you believe—" She stopped suddenly. Her whole body shuddered. Her hands were trembling.

I jumped up from the table. "Lizzy? Are you okay?"

A sob escaped her throat. "He's dead, Michael. Angel is dead. And now he's coming after us. I know it. He won't rest. He was an evil person when he was alive. I know he's much worse now. He won't stay in his grave until . . . until he's paid us back. Aren't you afraid? Aren't any of you afraid?"

She shuddered again. "I'm so frightened, so horribly frightened." Another loud sob burst from her throat and tears began to pour down her face.

Without thinking, I hurried forward, wrapped my arms around her, and hugged her tight. I was only thinking of stopping her from trembling.

But I glanced up and saw Pepper glaring at me, her face twisted in an angry scowl.

I held onto Lizzy. Her tears felt hot against my cheek.

Am I becoming obsessed with her?

The question flashed uninvited into my mind.

I don't know her at all. It's like . . . I've been hypnotized. I think about her all the time.

"Michael." Pepper's voice broke into my thoughts. "Michael, you and I—we have to talk."

21.

"I know, I know," I said. "I hugged Lizzy. I know why you're angry, Pepper."

She shook her head. "I'm not angry because you hugged her, Michael. I'm angry because you're a sucker. Because you're an idiot. Because you fell for all her phony garbage."

The others had left. We hadn't been able to decide anything. Gabe and Kathryn voted for calling the police and telling them everything about Saturday. Diego and I were totally opposed. How would confessing to the police help us with the Angel situation?

We all argued for nearly an hour, then decided we weren't getting anywhere. Lizzy was the most frightened of all of us. Maybe because she knew about Angel from her old school. Maybe because she was totally convinced he was dead in the snow last Saturday.

She started talking about evil spirits in the graveyard again. Gabe and Diego shouted her down. She found her coat and stormed out of the house. That pretty much ended the discussion.

How did we leave it? I don't really know.

Now Pepper and I were in the den. Normally, we'd be cozy together in a corner of the big leather couch. But tonight, Pepper perched on the edge of the armchair across from me.

"She's playing you, Michael," Pepper said, tugging down the sleeves of her yellow sweater.

"She was really frightened," I insisted. "So—"

"She was acting. She likes attention. Can't you see that?"

"No," I started. "I don't think—"

"It's like you're totally blind," Pepper said, leaning toward me across the low coffee table. She picked up a stack of wooden coasters and started shuffling them between her hands. Her eyes stayed locked on mine. "'Oh, Lizzy, you poor sensitive thing. You're so frightened. Let me hug you till you feel better.'"

"You're being ridiculous," I said.

"*You're* the one who's ridiculous," she snapped. She slammed the coasters back onto the tabletop. "All her crazy talk about spirits on the loose and souls roaming around in the graveyard. Did you buy that, too? Did you believe that stuff, too?"

"Calm down, Pepper," I said, motioning with both hands. "You're losing it. Seriously."

"I know. I know," she said. "I'm the crazy one. I'm a redhead so that makes me temperamental and jealous and emotional, right? Do you only think in dumb clichés, Michael?"

"This isn't getting us anywhere," I said. "Would you like me to apologize for hugging her?"

"I'd like you to apologize for being a jerk. For not seeing that Lizzy will do anything to get your attention."

I let out a long sigh. "I'll say it one more time, Pepper. Lizzy was frightened. She wasn't putting on an act. You are wrong to accuse her. She was scared. This is a very scary situation."

Pepper jumped to her feet. Her knees bumped the coffee table and sent the coasters spilling onto the floor. For the first time, I saw that she had tears in her eyes. Angry tears. "If you'd rather be with her, I'll leave."

I stood up, too, surprised at how fast my heart was beating. I brought my face close to hers. "If you're going to be angry and jealous all the time," I said, "maybe you *should* leave!"

She lowered her eyes. "So we're breaking up?"

"It seems that way," I said. Weird thing to say. That didn't sound like me at all. I think I was too angry to think like myself.

"You really are a jerk." She always had to have the last word.

I watched her pull her coat from the front closet and hurry out of the house. She slammed the door behind her.

I stood there for a long time, staring at the door. Did I expect Pepper to return? To come back and apologize?

No. I knew better than that. I stood there staring straight ahead, trying to clear my head, clenching and unclenching my fists. And I found myself thinking about Lizzy. How she trembled when I hugged her. How warm her face felt against mine.

I'm not sure how long my phone buzzed. I was so lost in my thoughts, I didn't even feel it vibrating in my jeans pocket. Finally, I snapped alert and tugged it up to my ear. "Hello?"

"You killed me." A raspy, hoarse whispered voice.

I blinked. I pulled the phone from my ear so I could read the ID. But the screen had only one word: Blocked. "Who is this?" I said.

"Your worst enemy," was the hoarse reply.

"Wait—" I started. My mind was spinning. Gabe loved to play phone tricks. Was this one of his dumber ones?

"You killed me and left me in the snow." The whisper rattled in my ear, stopped my thoughts about Gabe. *"Now it's my turn."*

The phone nearly slid from my hand. I tightened my grip and pressed it hard against my ear. "Wait a minute," I said. "What do you mean? Let's talk about this."

A short pause. Then: *"Talk? You killed me, and now you want to talk?"*

"You can't be dead," I insisted. "What do you want? Why are you calling me?"

"Who should I start with?"

"Huh? I don't get it. What do you want?" My voice rose to a whine. I took a breath. And listened.

"Who will be the first to go?" he rasped. *"Who will be the first to pay for what you did?"*

"Whoa. Wait," I said. "Listen to me—"

"How about that cute girl with the black hair and big, dark eyes, that girl you're so hot for?"

I swallowed. "Huh? Lizzy? What are you going to do to Lizzy?"

Silence for a long moment.

Then the phone clicked off.

22.

I sat hunched over my laptop in the yearbook office, staring at a blank screen. I knew what I wanted to write about for the yearbook blog, but I couldn't think of a way to get started.

I'd left the door open, and I could hear the voices in the hall, the laughter, the scrape and slam of lockers, the shouts and conversations as everyone collected their stuff and cleared out.

"Hey, Michael—?"

I turned as Gabe poked his head in. "How's it going?" I said.

"You going home?" he asked. He had a rolled-up poster in one hand. Gabe's a pretty good artist. He's been painting since he was a kid. He'd hoped to get an art scholarship to Pratt in New York City, but that hadn't worked out.

"I have to stay and write the blog," I said. "Pepper and I were supposed to go through old yearbooks. You know.

For the hundredth anniversary. But I don't think she's speaking to me."

Gabe nodded. "And what did you decide to do about that guy calling you?"

I shrugged. "Guess I've been trying not to think about it."

"But he threatened you," Gabe said. "He threatened *all* of us."

I drummed my fingers on the tabletop. "I know you want me to go to the police, Gabe. But I don't want to start a whole big thing. It's our senior year. We've got one semester to go, and we're out of here. I don't think we should jeopardize everything. If we can keep it quiet . . ."

Gabe made a face. "We've been over this. None of us wants to get in trouble. No way. But if some crazy psycho is going to come after us . . ."

"That's just talk," I said. "The guy has seen too many movies. I don't know what his problem is, but why would he spend his time coming after us? He just gets a rush by calling people and acting tough."

Gabe studied me. "You don't sound so sure. You're just telling yourself what you want to hear."

"Now you're a shrink?" I said.

"Why don't you at least tell your dad?" Gabe asked.

Pepper barged through the door, shoving Gabe out of her way, an armload of old Shadyside High yearbooks in her hands. "Tell your dad what?" she demanded.

"You mean we're speaking?" I said.

She squeezed past me and dumped the books with a *thud* on the other end of the table. "No. Not speaking," she said. She shimmied out of her backpack and tossed it to the floor, narrowly missing my foot.

"Catch you later," Gabe said. He gave me a quick salute with the rolled-up poster, then vanished.

Pepper shook the hair off her face with a toss of her head. "Tell your dad what?"

"About Angel calling me and making threats last night."

"Kathryn told me about it," Pepper said. "So now I guess you believe Lizzy and think we should all be shaking and quaking and afraid to leave our houses? Oh, Lizzy was right. The evil spirit is out to get us."

"Did you take annoying lessons?" I snapped.

"I learned it from you."

I raised my hands to the laptop keyboard. "Give me a break. I'm trying to write the blog."

Pepper pulled out a wooden chair. She made it scrape against the floor as loudly as she could. "Since we are co-editors and are forced to work together, perhaps you could tell me what your blog post is about."

I shrugged. "Read it and find out."

She smiled. "In other words, you don't know what it's about. You don't have an idea in your head, do you. Too busy daydreaming about beautiful Lizzy?"

"I think we should have a truce," I said. "A truce of silence."

She slammed a yearbook on the table as hard as she could. The whole table shook. I pretended I didn't notice. I turned to my laptop screen and raised my fingers to the keyboard.

I had a vague idea of what I wanted to write about. I wanted to describe going to the cemetery to do tombstone rubbings and what it felt like to stand there among all the really old graves. I had this thought that a lot of the people who are buried there once walked the halls of this school and had their photos in the yearbook and . . . and . . .

Well, that's as far as I'd gotten in my thinking. I wasn't sure what point I wanted to make. Something about history being part of life today maybe. I had to admit it. I didn't have it together. My brain was a total muddle.

"Maybe I won't write a blog entry today," I muttered.

And just as I started to close the lid on the laptop, I heard noises in the hall. I heard running footsteps. Then a high, shrill scream. Then a hard *thud,* like something crashing to the floor. More footsteps, running hard.

And then a girl's frightened cry: "Somebody help her! Get help! She's been hurt!"

23.

I jumped up, knocking my chair over backward. I lurched out into the hall. I heard more screams for help.

I turned toward the sound and saw Emmy Moore, a junior I know, on her knees, her eyes wide with horror, her hands cupped around her mouth as she screamed.

"Emmy—?" I shouted. I lowered my gaze and saw that she was leaning over someone. A dark-haired girl. Flat on her back, arms and legs spread out. Not moving. Not moving.

For a few seconds, the scene became a blur. As if my eyes didn't want to accept what I was seeing. Then Emmy and the girl on the floor snapped back into focus. And I dropped down across from Emmy.

"Lizzy?" Her name spilled from my mouth in a voice I didn't recognize. "Oh, no. Lizzy?"

Her eyes were shut. I saw a cut on her forehead. A small puddle of dark blood had formed above her head. Fighting back my shock, I called her name a few more times, but she didn't respond.

"Some kids went to get the nurse," Emmy said in a trembling voice. She smoothed a hand over Lizzy's forehead. "I think she's knocked out." She raised her eyes to me. "Do you know her?"

I nodded. "Yes. She's new. Her name is Lizzy Walker. Did you see what happened?"

"No," Emmy said. "I was in the music room. I had to get some music for jazz band. I heard a commotion out here and . . . and I saw her on the floor when I came out. No one else around."

"I think I heard someone running away," I said.

Emmy's eyes went wide. "You mean—?"

I turned and saw Pepper standing behind me. She stared down at Lizzy, her mouth open in shock. "I don't believe this," she murmured. "Is she . . . Is she . . . ?"

Lizzy groaned. She opened her eyes. She recognized me after a few seconds. She reached both hands up and grabbed my arms.

"Michael," she whispered. She groaned again. "He . . . came up behind me. I only . . . I only got a glimpse of him."

She let go of one of my arms and rubbed her forehead. Then she stared at the blood on her hand. "My head," she whispered. "I have such a headache."

"You're cut," Emmy told her. "I don't think it's too deep. We sent for the nurse."

Lizzy shut her eyes. "I saw him for a second. Before . . . before he hit me. It was him. It was Angel."

I gasped. "No. He said on the phone—"

"He hit me with something," Lizzy whispered, squinting up at me, gazing at me with those huge eyes as if pleading for help. "I guess I went down. Then he was whispering in my ear. He was bending over me, whispering. He was crazy. I mean crazy, Michael. He kept repeating, 'One by one . . . One by one.' He said he was going to get us all one by one."

24.

Diego crushed a Coke can in his hand and threw it down. "So what did Lizzy tell the police?" he asked.

I rolled my eyes. "Please don't leave that on the dining room table," I said. "Give me a break. Go throw it in the trash."

He burped. "Okay, Mom." He pushed back from the table, gave the back of my head a slap, and headed to the kitchen.

"Is Lizzy okay?" Gabe asked. He didn't look up from the scene he was drawing. The black marker squeaked against the paper.

We were working on a project for Ms. Curdy's English class. We didn't want to write the usual tired essays about *Macbeth*. You know. How he was so weak and indecisive and his wife was so totally ambitious. Bor-ing.

So we were doing storyboards for a video game based on the play. Gabe is the best artist in the group. He actually wanted to be a comic book artist when he was younger.

So he was sketching out the scenes, and Diego and I were plotting it.

"Yeah. She has like a bruise on her forehead but the cut wasn't too deep," I said.

"And what did she tell the cops?" Diego asked again, carrying a new can of Coke.

"She didn't tell them the truth," I said. "She didn't want them to know about how we ran the guy over and left him for dead last Saturday. So she said he was a masked guy she didn't recognize. She said he was trying to rob lockers. She saw him and screamed and he knocked her down and took off."

"Nice lie," Diego said. He tilted the can to his mouth and took a long, noisy drink. "All to protect cutey boy here." He pinched my cheek really hard. "Must be true love."

"Shut up," I said, shoving his arm away. "This isn't funny. If that lunatic Angel means what he says—"

"What isn't funny?" Mom stepped into the dining room. She had her tall satiny red jewelry box in her hands.

"*Macbeth,*" I said quickly. "*Macbeth* is definitely not a comedy."

She set the jewelry box down at the other end of the table. "I played one of the witches in our college production at Middlebury," she said. "I still remember burning my hand on the dry ice in the witches' cauldron."

I think Mom remembers every time she hurt herself. A lot of her stories end with her being injured somehow. I suddenly thought of her story about how she broke her arm the first time she tried to ride a two-wheeler.

"Were you into theater?" Gabe asked her.

She blew a strand of hair off her forehead. "That's a long sad story. I wanted to be a theater major, but my parents said it was a waste of time and they wouldn't pay my tuition if I did it."

"So what did you major in?" Gabe asked.

Mom chuckled. "Philosophy."

We laughed, too.

"You don't mind if I clean my jewelry while you work, do you?" Mom asked. She sat down at the other end of the table and started pulling rings and earrings out of the box.

"We're up to the murder," Gabe said, reaching for a blank sheet of paper.

"What if we make it so the player can choose his victim?" Diego asked. "You know. Like who should Macbeth kill first? Maybe we give him an automatic rifle, and he runs through the castle—"

"We need to follow the play a little bit better," I said.

"But that's no fun," Diego protested. He shook his head. "Maybe this idea sucks."

Gabe frowned at Diego. "We've got a good start here. You never want to finish anything."

Diego shook a fist in Gabe's face. "I'll finish *you.*"

"Now, boys," Mom said. "Don't fight."

"Just joking," Diego said. He squeezed the back of Gabe's neck.

Mom had jewelry spread all over her end of the table. She held up a bracelet. "Look at this. If you don't polish silver, it all turns black. When was the last time I cleaned these?"

"What if Mrs. Macbeth has the rifle?" Diego said.

"It's not Mrs. Macbeth. It's *Lady* Macbeth," I said. Why did I bother to correct him?

Mom sighed. "I'm going to need more silver polish." She climbed to her feet and left the room.

One second later, the front door burst open and Lizzy came hurtling into the dining room, her coat open, her dark hair wild about her head.

"Didn't you see him?" she cried breathlessly.

The three of us turned to her. "See him?" I said.

"Angel," she said, holding her side, struggling to catch her breath. "Didn't you see him? I started to walk up the drive. I saw him. He was watching you through the window. He's out there. He's still out there!"

Gabe, Diego, and I didn't say a word. We jumped to our feet. I turned to the dining room window. Pale moonlight reflected on the glass. No one there now.

Without thinking, we took off. We ran past Lizzy, through the living room and out the front door. It was a clear, cold night. A big full moon hung low over the houses across the street, making the patches of snow on the front lawns glow as if in daylight.

I jumped off the front stoop, my breath puffing like small clouds above my head. I narrowed my eyes at the wide trunk of the old sycamore tree near the driveway. Was he watching from behind the tree?

"Angel?" I shouted. "Angel?" My voice came out muffled in the heavy cold air.

No answer. No sign of anyone.

I took a few steps down the lawn. My shoes thudded softly over the frozen ground. Gabe and Diego followed close behind.

A shadow moved by the side of the house. A cat? A raccoon?

"Angel? Are you out here? Are you here?"

My shout was answered only by a rush of cold wind.

"No one here," I heard Gabe murmur.

And then I felt strong hands close around my neck. I felt the powerful hands grab me from behind. The fingers tightened . . . tightened . . . until a choking sound escaped my throat.

"Ohh." I uttered a helpless cry as my attacker bumped me hard from behind, wrapped his arms around my waist, and tackled me to the ground.

25.

I landed hard on my shoulder. Pain shot down my arm, down my whole body. I groaned.

He slid off me. I squirmed away, rolled onto my back. And stared up at my grinning friend. "Diego—you really are a jerk."

He reached both hands down to help me up. "Thought I'd give you a little thrill, Scout."

I shoved his hands away and jumped to my feet, both fists tight at my sides. "That wasn't funny. We've got a real problem here."

"Sorry," he said, but the grin was frozen on his face. "The suspense was killing me. So I thought we needed some action." He laughed. "Love that gurgling sound you made. Could you do that again?"

I swung my fist at him, but he dodged it easily. It made him laugh harder.

Gabe shook his head. "Michael is right. That wasn't funny, Diego. If that creep is out here . . ."

I rubbed my shoulder. The pain still throbbed down my arm. I glared at Diego. "Why do I put up with you?"

He shrugged his big shoulders. "Because I'm funny?"

I shoved him with both hands. "Because I have no taste in friends." Still trying to rub the pain from my shoulder, I led the way back into the house.

Lizzy was still in her coat. She stood tensely at the front door. "Well? Did you see him?"

"He must have run when you arrived," I said.

Mom was back at her place at the dining room table. "Why did you boys run out?" she called.

The three of us exchanged glances. "I . . . uh . . . thought I left something in my car," Gabe said, thinking quickly.

Mom raised her gaze from the bracelet she was polishing. "And all three of you had to go out to look for it?"

Gabe hesitated. "Well . . . it's hard to find things in the dark," he said finally.

Mom stared at him. "What was it you forgot?"

"I don't know," Gabe said. "We couldn't find it."

I laughed really hard to try to cover up what a stupid answer that was.

She narrowed her eyes to study us. She sniffed the air. "You didn't go outside to smoke, did you?"

I rolled my eyes. "Sure, Mom. We like to smoke in the freezing cold and the snow without any coats on. I smoked a whole pack while I was out there."

She made a face at me. "Sarcasm is the lowest form of humor. Did anyone ever tell you that?"

"You have," I said. "But only a hundred times."

Shaking her head, she returned to her jewelry. Gabe, Diego, and I sat down at the other end of the table by Gabe's drawings. "Let's get back to *Macbeth*," I said. "We're up to the murder, remember?"

A chill rolled down my back. I raised my eyes to the window. No one peering in at us.

Do I have to be afraid every day now?

Lizzy tossed her coat onto the living room couch and came into the room, brushing down her hair with both hands. She walked over to my mother and gazed at the jewelry spread out on the table. "Can I help you?"

"Sure," Mom said. "Let me go get another cloth and you can help polish some of these."

As soon as Mom was out of the room, Lizzy turned to us. "I saw Angel earlier today, too," she confided in a low voice. "He was standing across the street from the high school. Leaning against a tree. Just standing there in that long black overcoat, watching everyone leave the school building. I could hear him cursing to himself. He didn't see me. I turned and hurried the other way."

"We need to call the police," Gabe said. "I keep saying this over and over but no one listens to me."

"I'm with Gabe now," Diego said. "I've changed my mind. That nut has already hurt Lizzy. He—"

"We have to think of our future," I interrupted. "I'm as scared of this guy as you are. But we don't want the police to know—" I stopped because my mom returned to the room.

Lizzy took a chair near her and began polishing a silver pin. Us three guys tried to get back to our game story-boards, but it was hopeless. We'd lost the mood. And maybe the whole thing wasn't such a hot idea anyhow.

"What if we mix *Macbeth* with something else?" Diego suggested. "You know. Like *The Avengers*. We could prob-ably make a better game. More action."

"Ms. Curdy loves Shakespeare," I said. "I don't think she's into *The Avengers.*"

"There's plenty of action in *Macbeth,*" Mom said, hold-ing a large brooch up to the light. "You could do a hand-washing game." She realized that idea was greeted by total silence. "Okay, okay. I'll shut up."

A short while later, Gabe and Diego left, discouraged, depressed. We hadn't finished our storyboards. We didn't even agree that it was a good idea anymore.

Mom thanked Lizzy for her help. She collected her jew-elry and replaced it all carefully in the red box. Then she carried it upstairs. She and Dad watch *Law & Order* every night at about this time.

Lizzy and I drifted into the living room. I thought she was going to pick up her coat, but instead she turned to me. She pressed her pointer finger against mine. "We're bloods, remember?" she said softly.

And then she wrapped her arms around me, brought my head down, and pressed her lips against mine. Startled, it took me a few seconds to respond. Her lips moved over mine, pressing harder, a long probing kiss, so long I found it hard to breathe. But when I tried to pull my face back, she held the back of my head with both hands and pushed me against her, and we held the kiss until we were both breathless.

Finally, she let her hands slide from my hair. My heart pounding, I could still taste her lips on mine. She didn't say a word. She leaned over the couch and picked up her coat.

"Let me drive you home," I said.

"No, I'll be fine."

"No. Really," I insisted.

"I don't have far to go, Michael."

I realized I didn't know where she lived.

She pressed our fingers together again. I had an impulse to grab her and try to repeat that amazing, endless kiss. But she turned away from me and escaped out the front door without another word.

I watched her trot down the driveway, over patches of snow, to the sidewalk. She didn't look back.

In my room five minutes later, I got another call from Angel.

26.

"ello, Michael. Have you been thinking of *me*?"

"Angel? Were you at my house? Were you here?" My voice came out higher than I'd anticipated. I didn't want to sound that afraid, but my mouth suddenly felt dry as cotton.

"So you *have* been thinking of me," he said in his raspy whisper.

"I want you to leave me alone," I said through gritted teeth. "I want you to leave my friends alone, too."

"The way you left me alone in the snow?" he replied. "The way you left me there and rode away after you killed me?"

"Obviously, I didn't kill you—" I started.

"Listen to me, you jerk." He began to lose his temper. The whisper became a growl. "You killed me. Why would I lie? Didn't you and your buddies come visit my new home, the graveyard?"

"That's crazy," I said. "I saw you there, but—"

"Shut up and listen. It's my turn. You all have to pay for what you did. One by one . . . One by one."

I took a deep breath. I pressed the phone to my ear. "No! That's enough, Angel. You have to stop."

"Stop? Stop?" He laughed, a cold mirthless laugh. "How can I stop? I just got *started*."

"No. No way." Somewhere I found the courage to stand up to this psycho.

"Who will be next?" he said. "I took care of that cute girl you're so into. But that was just a love tap. I can do better work than that. You'll see."

I pictured Lizzy out cold on her back in the hall, her hair spread under her, blood seeping from the cut on her head. "Wait—" I said. "Please—"

"Watch your lunch bag, Michael."

I wasn't sure I heard him correctly. "Excuse me?"

"Watch your lunch bag. Watch for it, okay?"

"What lunch bag?" I cried. "I don't carry—"

"Later, alligator." He clicked off.

I let out a growl. Then I tossed my phone across the room. It landed on the bed and bounced into the wall. I felt like screaming and punching something as hard as I could. Somehow I felt more angry than frightened.

What am I going to do about him?

I didn't have time to think about it. A hard knock on my bedroom door startled me and made me spin around. "Yes?"

The door swung open slowly and Mom poked her head in. "Are you on the phone? Sorry."

"No. I'm off," I said. "What's up?"

Mom shook her head. "My amethyst ring is missing," she said. "I cleaned it and put it aside on the table. Now I can't find it anywhere."

I squinted at her. "You mean the ring you wear every day?"

She nodded. "Yes. My favorite."

"Did you look under the dining room table?" I asked. "Did you check the carpet. Maybe it fell—?"

"I checked everywhere. Every inch of the dining room. And I've been through my jewelry box three times. It just isn't there."

A picture flashed into my mind. Lizzy at the grocery store. The first time I ever saw her. Shoving cold cuts into her bag.

So much happened since then. That afternoon seemed like a long time ago. I thought of our long kiss as she held onto me so tightly and wouldn't let me go.

She wouldn't steal my mother's ring—would she?

27.

"Tell me again about your *Macbeth* project," Ms. Curdy said.

Kathryn poked me in the ribs. I was lucky she sat beside me in this first period class. She could always poke me and wake me up or shake me out of my daydream.

I definitely hadn't been listening to Ms. Curdy. I was thinking about Lizzy. I came to school early, hoping to catch her at her locker. But I didn't see her, and she wasn't in homeroom. I kept watching for her, thinking maybe she overslept and would sneak into school late. But it was close to nine and she hadn't appeared in English class.

"Your project, Michael?" Ms. Curdy repeated. Perched on the edge of her desk, she leaned forward and peered at me through her rimless glasses. She is a small, thin woman, in her fifties, I think. She has wavy gray hair parted in the middle, very pale skin, a nice smile. She wears mostly woolly ski sweaters and long skirts that come down almost to her ankles, and everyone likes her because she's smart and funny and she's a real easy grader.

I cleared my throat. Kathryn was preparing to poke me again.

"Well . . . we're kind of planning a video game," I said. "Based on the play. Diego, Gabe, and I. We're doing storyboards. You know. Mapping the whole game out."

Ms. Curdy twitched her nose at me. The fluorescent ceiling lights reflected in her glasses. I couldn't see her eyes. "You're doing that for extra credit?" she asked.

I shook my head. "No. That's our project. Instead of an essay. We thought—"

"Nice try, guys," she said. "That's a very creative way to get out of writing your essays."

"But—but—" I sputtered. "The game will show our interpretation of the play. You see—"

Ms. Curdy laughed. "Why don't you sell me the Brooklyn Bridge?" she said.

I leaned forward in my seat. "Excuse me?"

"If you think I'll buy that bull, why don't you try to sell me the Brooklyn Bridge, too?"

Now the whole class was laughing. For some reason, Kathryn thought it was hilarious. She has a weird sense of humor. I guess you have to have a weird sense of humor to go out with Diego.

I waited till things quieted down. "So you're saying . . . ?"

Ms. Curdy smiled her toothy smile. "I'm saying I can't

wait to read your essays. And if you guys want to create that game about the play for extra credit, that would be awesome, too."

I nodded.

"I only say the word *awesome* so I'll sound young to you people," she said. "I don't really say it at home."

I didn't know how to respond to that. I nodded again. All I knew was, Diego, Gabe, and I had just been shot down. We had wasted a lot of time, and there was no way we'd finish those storyboards now.

I mean, we didn't need extra credit. We were seniors. We were halfway out of there.

The rest of the morning went okay. We were doing gymnastics in Phys. Ed., and it helped to wake me up. I have lunch fourth period, which is kind of early, around eleven thirty, but I'm usually hungry by then anyway.

On my way to the lunchroom, I stopped to talk to Kerry Reacher and Eric Finn, two friends of mine. They were planning some kind of pregraduation party, like six months early. "To get the partying started," Eric said. "I mean, what's the point of waiting?"

Kerry thought it would be cool to have a whole day with the snowmobiles. Except most of the snow melted this week. I told them if we get another really good snow, I could talk to my dad about it.

Thinking about snowmobiles made me feel tense, though. I wondered if I'd ever be able to enjoy being on one again, if I'd ever be able to just have the kind of fun I used to have and not think about that nut Angel and not picture slamming into him and sending him flying.

"You killed me, Michael."

I could hear his raspy whisper in my head. I heard those words a lot.

"You killed me, Michael."

I could smell the food from the lunchroom. Sometimes they have these really good pizza bagels. They're so small, I have to grab at least six of them, but they're really tasty.

I was stepping up to the doorway when Kathryn appeared again and blocked my path. "What's up?" I said.

Her hazel eyes peered into mine. "It isn't true—is it?"

I blinked. "Huh?"

"Tell me it isn't true."

"Okay," I said. "It isn't true. I don't know what you're talking about, Kathryn. But it isn't true."

I tried to edge around her, but she slid in front of me. "Did you really give that ring to Lizzy?" she asked.

That got my attention.

"Ring? What ring?"

Kathryn tossed her hair back. "The one she's wearing on a chain around her neck. An amethyst ring. She's showing it off and telling everyone you gave it to her."

28.

I must have gone pale or something because Kathryn grabbed me by the shoulders. "Are you okay?"

For a moment, the whole lunchroom and everyone in it became a blur, all out of focus. Then it all turned red. Angry red. I actually saw red!

"She can't do that!" I screamed.

A bunch of kids turned around to see who was shouting. I didn't care. I felt so angry, I thought my head might burst open.

I realized Kathryn was still holding onto me, her face filled with concern. "What's up, Michael? You didn't give Lizzy the ring?"

"It . . . it's a misunderstanding," I said.

What was I supposed to do? Tell Kathryn that Lizzy stole my mother's ring? That she's showing it off now? Telling everyone I gave it to her? Even though it's a total lie, and she stole it?

Kathryn let go of me, but her eyes kept studying mine. "So are you going to tell me?"

"Later. Kind of a long story," I murmured. I really didn't want to go into it with Kathryn. I had to straighten it out with Lizzy. I had to confront her and find out why she would do such a crazy thing. I didn't say a word the afternoon I saw her shoplifting food. But this was different.

"Have you seen Lizzy?" I asked, my eyes surveying the crowded room, moving from table to table. "She wasn't in homeroom this morning. Where is she?"

Kathryn shrugged. "I think she came in late. I ran into her on the second floor near the art room. She was seriously excited. She backed me into a corner and showed me the ring around her neck. When she told me you gave it to her last night, I . . . well . . . I didn't know what to say. I thought you and Pepper . . . I thought you two would probably make up. I didn't know you have such a thing about Lizzy."

"It's messed up," I said. My stomach growled. I started to feel weird again. Everything started to blur. "Catch you later, okay?"

Kathryn nodded and made her way out of the lunchroom. I didn't really feel like eating. My stomach was tight as a knot. But I started to the cafeteria line.

The period was nearly over. Only a few kids in line. A few sandwiches left. Some tired-looking chicken in cream sauce. I was too late for the pizza bagels. That tray was empty.

I was trying to decide what to do when I felt a light tap on my shoulder. I turned to see a girl I didn't know. She was cute, with round blue eyes and a short blonde ponytail. She must have been a ninth-grader because she looked about twelve.

"Hi," I said.

She handed me a brown paper lunch bag. "This is for you," she said. She shoved it into my hand.

I couldn't hide my surprise. "What? I don't understand. I—"

"That guy told me to give it to you." She pointed to the front of the room.

I saw two girls heading to the exit, but I didn't see a guy there.

"Hey, he's gone," she said. She turned back to me. "Guess he brought your lunch?"

"I don't know," I said. I raised the bag. It was light. It felt empty. Not heavy enough to have a sandwich or anything inside.

"Well, bye." She turned and walked away, her ponytail swinging behind her.

Angel warned me about a lunch bag, I remembered. *Is this it?*

I turned it in my hands as I carried it to an empty table in the corner. Someone called to me from across the room but I didn't stop to reply.

I dropped onto the edge of the table and unfolded the top of the bag. I saw two words scrawled in big jagged letters in red marker on the side of the bag. *You're next.*

My hand trembled as I opened the bag and peered inside. At first, I couldn't tell what I was looking at. Some kind of fluffy material? I reached into the bag and pulled out a chunk of it.

It was copper-colored, sort of orange-red. Very soft. A clump of hair. Yes. Yes . . .

I finally realized what I was holding.

I dug my fingers into the bag and pulled out a bigger sample.

Hair. The bag was filled with coppery red hair.

I squeezed a clump of it. Let it sift through my fingers.

Then I dropped the bag and jumped to my feet as I realized what I was holding.

Pepper's hair. The bag was packed full with Pepper's hair.

29.

Shadyside General Hospital is located on the River Road, a few miles past my dad's snowmobile store. After school, I reached Pepper's mother on the phone, and she told me that Pepper was there being treated for trauma. She'd probably have to stay overnight.

I had a million questions, but I didn't ask them. I said I was on my way and clicked off the phone. I hurried home to get Mom's car.

It had been snowing all day, the temperature was about fifteen, and the roads in my neighborhood hadn't been cleared yet. Icy slick. But I was eager to get to the hospital and see how Pepper was doing.

It took me awhile to scrape ice off the windshield and back window. I was backing down the driveway, tires crunching over the fresh snow, when I saw someone trotting toward my house, waving both arms in the air.

I braked. The car slid back a few inches before stopping. Gabe knocked on my window with his gloved hand. I rolled the window down. He was breathing hard from running, his breath puffing up in front of him.

"I'm going to the hospital," I said.

He nodded. His blue wool ski cap was pulled down almost over his eyes. His face was red from the cold. "I heard about Pepper. I'll come with you."

He ran around to the other side of the car, tossed his backpack onto the backseat, and climbed in next to me. "I heard she was attacked."

The car crunched down the drive and into the street. "I'm pretty sure it was that psycho Angel," I said. I started to turn onto Park Drive. The car slid sideways, tilting hard to the right. I kept tapping the brake, moving the wheel till I got it back in control.

"This is going to be a thrill ride," Gabe said, adjusting his seatbelt.

"Maybe the plows have already cleared the River Road," I said, slowing for a red light.

"Did you talk to Pepper?"

I shook my head. "No. Her mom. She said Pepper wasn't badly hurt. But she's very upset. I think she's still a little bit in shock."

"What does that mean?" Gabe rubbed his window with a gloved hand. "In shock. I always wondered what that means."

"I think it means your brain just can't adjust to what's happening to you," I said.

Gabe's expression turned serious. "So did the guy drag Pepper off somewhere and cut off her hair? Did he knock her out first?"

"I don't know," I said. "I didn't want to stay on the phone with her mom. I wanted to get over there."

Gabe shook his head. "Now we have no choice. We really have to tell the police about Angel."

Huge snowflakes bombarded the windshield as the snow began to come down again. It was four in the afternoon but nearly as dark as night. The headlights reflected off a curtain of blowing snow.

I sighed. "Guess you're right, Gabe."

We passed my dad's store and started the curving climb up the River Road with its sharp turns and steep cliffs on the right. Being back here reminded me of our Saturday snowmobile party that had ended so badly. Once again, I felt the crash of my snowmobile into Angel, and once again I saw his dark overcoat and his startled expression as he went flying into the air from the impact.

"You killed me, Michael."

Headlights of oncoming cars filled the windshield with yellow light, making it even harder to see. Snow swirled around the car, the wind howling. I felt as if we were driving inside a tornado.

Gabe was saying something about *Macbeth,* but I was concentrating too hard on my driving and worrying about Pepper, and his words seemed like background music. I wasn't even trying to listen. I leaned forward as much as I could, squinting into the snow-blown windshield, gripping the wheel tightly in both hands.

And then I felt the bump from behind. My car jumped. Jumped then skidded a few feet.

Gabe's eyes went wide. "Someone hit us."

The road curved sharply. The headlights swept over the low guardrail.

"They must've slid," I said. "An accident."

"Are you going to stop?" Gabe asked.

Another hard *thud* sent the car sliding into the oncoming lane. My heart skipped a beat. I swung the wheel, swerved back. And another hard bump sent us shooting forward.

"It's not an accident!" Gabe cried.

I peered into the rearview mirror, trying to see the driver of the car behind us. But my back window was clogged with snow. I couldn't see a thing.

"Pull over!" Gabe cried. "Pull over. He's trying to *kill* us!"

"There's no place to pull over," I said, my voice trembling in fright. "No shoulder."

Bummmp.

A hard push from behind sent us skidding toward the guardrail and the cliff beyond it.

"No way! I don't believe this!" I cried angrily. I swung the wheel to the left, swung it hard, and the car slid back into the lane.

Gabe had his eyes shut, his hands clamped tightly together in his lap. "This isn't happening," he muttered. "Is it that crazy fool—?"

He didn't finish his question.

I gripped the wheel, slowed almost to a crawl, my foot poised over the brake. But being careful didn't help.

The next hard butt from the car behind sent us sliding fast. The guardrail loomed up from out of the darkness. The headlights swept over the low metal rail, and then the car slammed into it hard, with a shrill squeal of metal against metal.

We hit on Gabe's side. I saw him bounce in his seat. Saw his head jerk back. He uttered a startled groan.

And then the car scraped against the metal guardrail, sliding out of control, seeming to pick up speed. A grinding roar filled my ears. Like a scream. A scream of metal against metal. I spun the wheel. Spun it.

Too late.

Through the snow-smeared windshield, I saw the guardrail split and give way. The car slid through the opening. Sailed out. Sailed . . . as if taking off into the night sky.

The grinding roar stopped. Silence. For a moment, we were surrounded by nothing but a thick clotted blackness.

And then Gabe and I opened our mouths in screams of horror as the car nosed down, and we plunged off the cliffside, and dropped . . . dropped tumbling . . . somersaulting . . . to the rocky shore below . . . dropped into a darkness I had never seen or felt before.

30.

I woke up in the hospital. I felt groggy, the light shimmering on and off in my eyes. But I knew where I was instantly. I saw the tube in my arm and the clear bag of liquid on a pole beside my bed, and the beeping monitor against the wall. I knew where I was, and I was awake, but I wasn't sure I was ready . . . ready to talk to people . . . to face the world again.

How did I get here? How long have I been here? Am I okay? Is Gabe okay? Do my parents know?

The questions pressed down on my mind like heavy weights. Too many questions. . . . Too much horror. . . . Too much . . .

I sank back into the warm soft sheets and closed my eyes. After a while, I heard my parents' voices, soft murmurs nearby. One of them said, "I think Michael's waking up. I saw his eyes open." The other one whispered, "Thank God."

I felt a wave of happiness, knowing my parents were there with me. Happiness and relief. I was alive and my parents were with me.

I opened my eyes and cleared my throat. "Mom? Dad?"

As their faces appeared above me, it all flashed back in my memory. I remembered the terrifying feeling of flight as the car crashed through the guardrail and sailed into the sky. And I remembered our screams as we came tumbling down, remembered the jolts and the bangs, the rattle of metal, the crash of shattering glass, the shocks of pain, the total surprise of it all.

Mom and Dad leaned over the bed. Their eyes were red, their faces tired. Their cheeks were stained with tear tracks.

I blinked a few times. I tried to speak. But no sound came out. I was so glad to see them, I wanted to laugh and cry and shout at the same time.

It took a few seconds for them both to come into clear focus. I finally found my voice. "What did I break?" I asked. The question popped out of my mouth from out of nowhere. It startled even me.

Mom put her hands on the sides of my head. "You're okay, Michael. You didn't break anything. You're okay. And now you're awake. Awake, thank God."

I nodded. My head felt as heavy as a rock, but I had no trouble moving it up and down. My arms moved, and I could move my legs.

"You didn't break anything," Dad said. He had tears in his eyes. He made no effort to wipe them away. "The doctor said it was some kind of miracle. You seem to be unbreakable."

"You'll probably feel achy for a while," Mom said. "Your muscles are all strained and twisted. Physical therapy will take care of that. And you have a few bruises, Michael. But you didn't break any bones or anything."

She patted the covers on top of my chest. In the bright hospital light, I saw tears glistening on her cheeks, too. "You're okay. You're going to be okay," she repeated in a trembling voice.

"You're a lucky guy," Dad said. "The car was totaled. Do you remember how it happened?"

I nodded again. "I remember," I said. "But . . . I . . . I'm so sleepy. My head . . . I feel like I'm in a thick fog."

Mom patted my chest again. "It's okay. There will be plenty of time to talk."

"Yes. We'll talk later," Dad said. He took a few steps back from the bed.

"Can we get you something?" Mom said. "Are you hungry? Do you have an appetite?"

"I don't think so," I said. I shut my eyes. I started to fade into darkness again. But then I suddenly remembered. "Hey," I said. "Hey. You didn't tell me. Where is Gabe? How is he doing?"

The both took sharp intakes of breath. Mom went pale.

They exchanged glances. "Uh . . ." Mom opened her mouth to speak but stopped.

"I'm sorry, Michael," Dad said, avoiding my gaze. "Gabe didn't make it. He . . . he was crushed to death inside the car."

31.

Gabe.

The next two days in the hospital were so strange. I would sleep and wake up not sure why I was feeling so sad . . . and then I would remember Gabe. Gabe, my best friend . . . where is he?

Then I would remember. Gabe is dead. I said it over and over, but it didn't seem possible. How do you ever get over losing your best friend? At first, I just felt so sorry for Gabe . . . and for myself. But after a while, my sadness turned to anger. I wanted to get Angel. I wanted to make him pay. I wanted to *kill* him.

I knew it was time to come clean. Time to tell the police everything. Time to make sure Angel didn't hurt or kill anyone else.

The day I was released from Shadyside General, Pepper and I had an appointment with the police. Our parents were there, too. We all met at Pepper's house.

"The police will be here any minute," Pepper's dad said,

tugging at the sleeves of his gray sweats. He works at home, doing some kind of research for the Engineering Department at the community college, and I've never seen him dressed in anything but gray sweats.

He has a thick head with straight white hair, narrow blue eyes, his cheeks turn red a lot, and he can have a sharp sense of humor. He's normally relaxed and joking around, but this afternoon, he was quiet and his eyes kept darting around, tense and alert.

I sat between Mom and Dad on the Davis's long black leather den couch. Pepper's dad stood at the window, peering out through the curtains.

Pepper sat on the edge of an ottoman across from us, her hands clasped in her lap. She wore a soft blue floppy cap that covered her head. She said she didn't want anyone to see the cuts and bruises on her scalp. And the patches of hair that Angel hadn't cut, patches and clumps of red hair that now looked so ugly and sad.

She kept staring at me, her expression angry. "We're going to tell everything today. Yes, Michael?" she said.

"I had the feeling for quite awhile you've been keeping something from us," Mom said to me. "I don't know why. Just a feeling I had."

Dad's gaze went from Pepper to me. "I take it you both have a good idea why these things happened to you?"

"Here come the police," Mr. Davis said. He pushed back the window curtains and hurried to the front door. A few seconds later, he led two dark-uniformed officers into the den.

Officer Gonzalez was a tall, slim young woman with straight black hair tied behind her head in a long ponytail, dark serious eyes, and a no-nonsense expression. Her eyes took in the whole room as she entered.

She was nearly a foot taller than her partner, Officer Nova. He removed his cap, revealing a nest of curly gray hair. He had a round chubby face and a carefully trimmed black-and-gray mustache and goatee. He carried a small iPad in one hand and began typing on it as soon as we all introduced ourselves.

The two cops adjusted their gun holsters as they sat on the small couch across from us. Nova's belly strained the fabric of his shirt. He cleared his throat. "Who wants to start?"

"Tell us what you think is going on," Gonzalez said. "Take your time. Don't leave out any details. Officer Nova and I will decide what's important."

Pepper and I exchanged glances. So far, I'd managed not to tell my parents much of anything. They begged me to talk to them, but I never felt strong enough. . . .

I knew Dad would have a fit when he learned about the snowmobile accident. I wanted to put off telling him about it as long as I could. Now my hands were icy and wet and my heart was thumping like crazy in my chest. No more stalling.

"I think Michael should start," Pepper said. I thought I detected a little bitterness in her voice. Like what happened to her was all my fault.

And to tell the truth, I felt she was right.

I let out a long sigh. Then I began to tell them everything that had happened, starting with the snowmobile party that Saturday afternoon.

A hush fell over the room as I talked. For some reason, I grew more nervous as I went on. My throat tightened, my mouth felt dry as a desert, and I had to stop to get a sip of water.

My dad uttered a short cry of surprise when I described the snowmobile accident. "Michael, you should have told me," he interrupted. "You should have come to me. I would have gone with you to the police and maybe none of this would have happened." He seemed sad, not angry.

"I am so sorry, Dad," I murmured. "I know you're right. But . . . we didn't want to get into trouble, and . . . and . . . well, we just didn't know how much trouble there would be."

"Please continue, Michael," Gonzalez said, motioning with one hand. Nova kept typing on his iPad. "You're doing a good job."

"No more interruptions till he finishes," Nova said, gazing at my dad.

"Sorry," Dad muttered. "I just don't like surprises like that."

"There are more surprises," I said. I took another sip of

water and began again. I told how we left Angel in the snow because we thought he was dead, and then how we returned to find him gone.

"So he wasn't dead?" Nova asked, looking up from his iPad. "Or was he dead and now he's a zombie?"

Gonzalez frowned at her partner.

"Just asking," Nova said with a shrug.

"He started calling and making threats," I continued. "He said I killed him. I killed him and now he was going to pay us all back."

Nova stopped talking. "That's what he said? Did he sound like he was joking? Did he really think he was dead?"

"I don't know," I answered. "He kept saying I killed him. And . . . I saw him in the graveyard. My class was there. It was a real foggy day. I mean, you couldn't see very far at all. But I saw him in the graveyard, and it looked like he was climbing up from a grave."

Nova grunted. He muttered something under his breath. He turned to Pepper, who hadn't said a word the whole time. "Did you see this guy Angel in the graveyard? Were you there that morning?"

Pepper nodded. The big cap flopped forward over her forehead. "I was there but I didn't see him."

Everyone turned back to me. Beside me, Dad stared straight ahead, his face locked in an angry expression. I don't think he believed he was hearing this story. I had let him down. I had kept everything from him. And now he stared at the den wall, not looking at anyone.

"So this guy Angel is coming after us one by one," I said. "He called and warned me. He told me what he planned to do."

Gonzalez shook her head. "Michael, you're a smart boy, aren't you? Why did you keep this a secret? I can't believe you didn't call the police department. Or even tell your parents. You made a terrible mistake in judgment."

"I know," I said in a whisper. I lowered my head. I thought about Gabe. Would he still be alive if we had gone to the police when Angel's threats began?

Nova's eyes burned into mine. "You should have called us. Are you so afraid of your father that you couldn't tell him about hitting that guy?" He turned a suspicious eye on my dad.

"N-no," I stammered. "No. That wasn't it. I . . . just didn't want to get in trouble. We all thought—"

"Do you have this guy Angel's phone number on your phone?" Gonzalez interrupted.

I shook my head. "It came up 'Blocked.' There was no number."

"We may need to take your phone to the police lab," she said. "So he warned you he was coming?"

"Yes. He wouldn't listen to me. He wouldn't let me apologize or anything. He just kept saying I'd killed him and now he was going to get us. So . . . first he knocked out Lizzy at school. Then he attacked Pepper and cut off her hair. Then . . . then . . . he bumped me off the River Road. He tried to kill me."

My whole body shuddered. A cry escaped my throat. I couldn't help myself. I was totally losing it.

"Don't you see?" I cried. "It was supposed to be me. I was supposed to die when the car went over the cliff. But it was Gabe instead. He . . . he wasn't supposed to be there. It was supposed to be *me*. Do you know how horrible I feel?"

Tears rolled down my cheeks. I couldn't stop my body from shaking. I saw that Pepper had turned away. She was crying, too.

Dad turned on the couch and put his arms around me. He hugged me tightly, whispering, "Take it easy. Just take a breath. You're okay."

Sure, *I* was okay. But I'd lost my best friend. And it was all my fault. If only we had gotten help for Angel and not run away. . . .

It took a few minutes to get myself together. Pepper had her hands over her face. Her cap slipped and I saw an ugly red scab on the side of her scalp.

"I don't think I have anything more to say," I told the two officers. "I've told you everything I know."

"Let's talk about this guy Angel," Gonzalez said. "First of all, what's his last name?"

Pepper and I stared at each other. "I don't know," we said in unison.

"We don't know anything about him," Pepper said. "This girl who was with us that Saturday . . . She told us his name was Angel. She said he used to go to her old school, but he got kicked out for beating up some people or something."

"So he probably has a record," Nova said. "We need his last name."

"Lizzy probably knows it," I said.

Gonzalez raised her eyes to me. "Lizzy?"

I nodded. "Lizzy Walker. She was the one who recognized him in the snow that afternoon. And she was the first one he attacked."

"Lizzy Walker," Nova murmured, typing. "We need to talk to her right away."

"Do you have a phone number for her?" Gonzalez asked.

I swallowed. I thought hard. "No. No, I don't. She . . . never called me. She said she didn't have a phone. Couldn't afford one."

Pepper squinted at me. "And she never called you on any phone or texted you?" Again, I heard the bitterness in her voice.

I shook my head. "I'm sorry. I don't have a phone number. She's new. She just moved here. We've only known her for a couple of weeks."

"Email?" Nova asked.

"No," I said. "She never emailed me. I . . . I don't have it."

Pepper stared at me suspiciously. Did she think I was lying? Covering up for Lizzy for some reason? "I'm telling the truth," I said to her.

"So you don't have her phone or email," Nova said. "Do you know where she lives?"

"S-she said it was near here," I stammered. "But . . . no. I don't know her address."

They turned to Pepper. "Don't look at me," she said. "I was never invited to her house. Believe me. We weren't friends."

Nova rubbed his goatee and studied Pepper. "Were you two enemies?"

"No way," Pepper answered quickly. She glanced at her father, who stood at the window watching in silence this whole time. "Michael and I . . . we were going out. Then Lizzy appeared and . . . started coming on to him. And . . . we broke up."

Nova nodded. "And she identified this guy Angel when he was lying there in the snow?"

Pepper nodded. "She said he was a psycho. That he beat up a teacher at her old school. Shoved his head through a glass door."

Nova turned to Gonzalez. "We have to talk to this girl . . ." He glanced at his iPad. ". . . Lizzy Walker. Right away."

"We'll get her contact information from the high school," Gonzalez said.

They both climbed to their feet. "We'll find this Angel guy," Gonzalez said.

Mr. Davis stepped away from the window. He gestured

to Pepper and me. "What should they do in the meantime? I mean, are they safe? Should we—?"

"You can go back to school," Gonzalez said. "We are going to set up a regular patrol there. But don't stay out late. Don't go out by yourselves. Try to stay in a group."

"Be careful," Nova said. "be *very* careful."

32.

It snowed nearly a foot on Friday night, the kind of snow that's crusty and hard on top and makes great cracking sounds when you walk on it. When the sun came out, the snow made the whole town sparkle.

Saturday afternoon I went to help out at Dad's store. We rode there in near silence. The River Road had been plowed, but our car still slid as we curved uphill. Dad had his country music station on, and he turned it up loud, I guess so he wouldn't have to talk to me.

He didn't even tell me that he got two awesome new Polaris Switchbacks in the store. I was dying to try one out. I mean, these beauties will go anywhere. They *dominate*.

But I knew better than to even ask him. It was going to take a long time before he would ever trust me again. He'd been very quiet all week. He didn't act angry or give me any long lecture or sit me down and have a man-to-man talk. He just said he was disappointed.

Mom said he was more frightened than angry. Sure, he

was upset that I didn't confide in Mom or him, even when I was in major trouble. But Dad was grateful I was alive and okay. Both my parents realized how close I'd come to dying . . . and that the guy who deliberately caused the accident was still somewhere out there.

The store was busy, mainly because everyone wanted to take advantage of the fresh snow. I worked the cash register in front for a while. Then I helped some new customers understand the difference between the sleds.

I kept checking my phone. I thought maybe I'd hear from Lizzy. I hadn't seen her or heard a word from her since that night at my house when she stole my mother's ring.

Should I have mentioned that to the police?

It didn't seem relevant. I mean, it didn't have anything to do with finding Angel and capturing him. And, I guess I still had some kind of weird hope that she'd have an explanation for me. I couldn't get that long kiss out of my mind . . . the way she held the back of my head and pressed herself against me so desperately . . .

I didn't want her to be a thief. I didn't want to get her in trouble. I'm not the kind of guy who gets lost in all kinds of crazy daydreams. Ask anyone. They'll tell you I'm totally down-to-earth, a no-nonsense type, I guess. But I had daydreams about Lizzy.

In fact, I couldn't get her out of my mind.

So why wasn't she getting in touch? Why hadn't she come around? She must have heard about the accident? She must have heard about Gabe.

A middle-aged couple, bundled up in matching blue down parkas and hoods as if we were in Alaska, rented a couple of the Arctic Cats. I took their credit card and swiped it through the machine. The man said something about this being their first time.

I nodded but I barely heard him. I told myself to concentrate on the store. But that wasn't easy.

I returned home around five and found Diego and Kathryn waiting for me in the living room. Mom had given them hot chocolate with marshmallows on top, and they were seated side by side, white mugs between their hands, on the green couch.

I tossed my coat on a chair and walked into the room. "Hey, what's up?"

Kathryn's hair fell around her face, as if it hadn't been brushed. She wore a blue-and-red ski sweater over a short blue skirt over black leggings. Diego was in a typical outfit for him, a huge maroon-and-gray Shadyside High sweatshirt and faded cargo jeans.

"Your mom said you were at the store," Kathryn said. "Everything okay?"

I think Kathryn took Gabe's death harder than any of us. I didn't think they'd been that close. But it was the idea that someone we were close to, someone we saw every day, could suddenly be gone. Gone forever.

Kathryn looked on the verge of tears. Diego had a hot chocolate mustache on his upper lip. He made no attempt to wipe it off.

I dropped down in the armchair across from them. "The store was crazy. You know. Fresh snow. Everyone wants to ride on it."

"The last time we were on snowmobiles was the last time we were happy," Kathryn said, lowering her eyes to the hot chocolate mug in her lap.

Diego slid his arm around her shoulders, trying to comfort her. "Did you hear any more about that creep?" he asked me. "Did the police find him? Have you heard anything at all?"

I shook my head. "Not a word."

"What are we supposed to do while we wait?" Kathryn asked, her voice cracking. "I mean, are we supposed to pretend everything is okay? Are we supposed to act normal, as if a crazed lunatic isn't out there, trying to kill us all?"

I didn't have a chance to reply. A loud knock on the front door made us all turn. I jumped up and hurried to the door. I gazed out the living room window but it was pretty much frosted over, so I couldn't see who it was.

Mom and I reached the door at the same time. I pulled it open and stared at a police officer. The sky had darkened to evening, and the porch light wasn't on. It took me a few seconds to recognize Officer Gonzalez standing in the dark blue haze.

She had her police cap on with earmuffs down, covering part of her face. "May I come in?"

Mom and I stepped aside so she could enter. She stamped

her snowy boots on the WELCOME mat. She pulled off her black gloves and stuffed them into the pockets of her coat.

"Sorry to interrupt," she said.

"Do you have news for us?" Mom asked.

"Not really," Gonzalez said. She saw Kathryn and Diego, standing tensely in the living room. "Oh, good. More of your friends are here." She started toward them, and Mom and I followed.

"Maybe one of you can give me some more information about this girl Lizzy Walker," Gonzalez said.

"Why?" I asked. "You said you were going to contact the school and—"

Officer Gonzalez locked her eyes on mine. "The school has no record of a Lizzy Walker," she said. "No record at all."

PART FOUR

PRESENT DAY

33.

I woke up the next morning with Lizzy on my mind. My dream lingered with me. In the dream, I was talking to Lizzy on the phone. That was the whole dream. I could see both of us at the same time. It was like we were in the same room, but we were having this long phone conversation.

As I blinked the sleep from my eyes, I couldn't remember what we talked about. The dream began to fade away, and I sat staring at the flapping window curtains. My room was freezing cold. I didn't remember leaving the window open.

I glimpsed my phone, plugged into the charger on my desk across the room. Why hadn't I ever talked to Lizzy on the phone? Why hadn't we texted one another?

She doesn't have a phone, I remembered. *She said she couldn't afford one.* I pictured her shoplifting food in the supermarket that day. "Maybe she's poor," I murmured to myself.

But if she was poor, how could she live here in North Hills, the most expensive neighborhood in Shadyside?

Or . . . maybe she doesn't.

I remembered how she refused to let me drive her home the other night. The first night she showed up at my house, she said she was lost. She lived only a couple of blocks away.

She could have been lying. But . . . why? "Maybe she's a runaway," I told myself.

Or maybe she's crazy.

She stole my mother's ring and showed it off in school. That's insane behavior. I pictured her pricking my finger with that pin that day in school. "We're bloods now," she said.

We're bloods—but I don't know a single thing about her.

I took a quick shower, still thinking about Lizzy. I pulled on jeans and a T-shirt and a sweater. I could smell coffee from the kitchen downstairs. And eggs. Mom liked to make scrambled eggs in the morning. I was pulling on my snow boots, thinking about the walk to school, when my phone dinged.

A message. I picked it up and read the screen:

Maybe you need driving lessons. Help prevent accidents.

My mouth dropped open. Angel.

I stared at the screen, gripping the phone close to my face. Was he going to write more?

No. That was the only message.

I jumped up with only one boot on. "Hey, Mom! Dad!" I shouted. I hobbled to the stairway. "Hey—look at this."

I made my way down to the kitchen. Dad was at the table, a plate of scrambled eggs in front of him, coffee mug nearly empty. Mom turned from the stove, a metal spatula in one hand. "Michael? What is it?"

I showed them the text from Angel. They stared at it open-mouthed.

"Maybe it can be traced," Dad said. He tugged his phone from his pants pocket. "I have that cop Gonzalez's direct number in my phone."

He punched in her number and waited. Shaking her head, Mom turned back to the eggs on the stove. Dad began telling Gonzalez about the text from Angel. I think she was giving him instructions on how to see if it could be traced to a phone number. Dad kept moving to different screens, but they all came up with one word: Blocked.

Scowling, he handed me back my phone. "Yes, we're all scared, Officer," he said. "That psycho is still out there. Still threatening my son. Of *course* we're scared." He listened to her for a while. "You're not reassuring me," he said. "He's still taunting. He's still texting. He isn't afraid of you. And you've made no progress at all."

She said something and then I heard her click off. Dad sat there, staring angrily at his phone.

"Your eggs are getting cold," Mom told him. "There's nothing more you can do right now."

Dad muttered some words under his breath. Mom lowered a plate of eggs in my place at the table. I didn't feel much like eating, but I didn't want to start an argument about it. She takes her eggs seriously. So I sat there with one boot on and forced myself to eat as much as I could.

Homeroom is at eight thirty, so I left the house a little before eight fifteen. It had started to snow again. There was already a fresh layer on top of the crusty snow that had already fallen. I crunched my way down the driveway and turned toward school. Across the street, Mr. Northrup's SUV had about a foot of snow on its roof. Two young men were shoveling the driveway of the Millers's house on the corner. The scrape of their shovels was the only sound except for the crunch of my boots as I made my way through the snow.

Mission Street hadn't been plowed yet. A single set of tire tracks dented the snow in the middle of the street. I didn't see any cars moving up or down the street.

Leaning into the blowing snow, I tugged my parka hood lower and trudged onto Park Drive. The wind howled through the wooded lot on the corner. I had my head down and didn't see the person step out of the trees until I nearly walked right into her.

Lifting my eyes, I saw a red parka. Then large snowflakes falling on black hair, loose about her face.

"Lizzy!" I cried.

34.

I had this sudden weird feeling that she wasn't real. That this was part of my lingering dream. She was a blur of red in the shimmering curtain of falling snow. Her head was uncovered, her hair flowing down the back of her parka, and her dark eyes seemed too large, too dark and too deep, peering so hard at me through the tumbling snowflakes.

"Lizzy?"

She grabbed my sleeve with a gloved hand. She was real. "Michael," she whispered. "Michael." She brushed snow from her hair with her free hand.

"Lizzy, what are you doing here? Are you coming to school?" My voice was muffled by the heavy frigid air.

She held onto my sleeve. Her breath steamed against my face. "Michael, you have to help me." Those amazing eyes pleaded with me.

"Help you? Lizzy, the police—they're looking for you."

She didn't react to my words. "It's Angel, Michael. You

197

have to help me. He's not through killing. He says you have more friends. He cannot let them live. He—he's so sick. He says that he's going to kill *me*." She pressed her cold cheek against mine. "Help me. Please."

"I can't help you," I said. "I'm frightened, too." I put my hands on the shoulders of her parka and pushed her back a few inches. "Lizzy, listen to me. You have to go to the police."

"I-I can't," she stammered. She wiped snow from her forehead.

"You have to," I insisted. "They're looking for you. They'll help protect you and everyone else."

She shook her head violently. Her expression became angry. "Don't be stupid, Michael. If I talk to the police, Angel will kill me. I know he will."

"But what can I do?" I said. "You have to help the police find him."

"No!" she cried. She grabbed my arm again and squeezed it hard. "We're bloods, remember? We're bloods. You gave me your ring, Michael."

"Whoa. Wait a minute," I said. "That ring—"

I couldn't finish. She grabbed the back of my head and pulled me to her. She pushed her lips against mine and kissed me, a desperate kiss that seemed like an attack. Her lips were surprisingly warm.

I tried to push back, but I came under her spell again. I couldn't resist her. I wanted to kiss her. I wanted to kiss her and kiss her. When she held me like that, I couldn't think straight. Like I lost my mind. Like I lost all sense. Like my brain was hijacked and I was floating off the ground and had left the real world behind.

She held me tighter and pressed her body against mine. I raised my hands and buried my fingers in her silky, dark hair.

When the kiss finally ended, we were both shivering, breathing hard, our breath puffing together into small clouds.

I swallowed. I could still taste her lips on mine.

"What do you want me to do, Lizzy?" The words burst out of me as if I wasn't saying them. "What do you want? I'll do *anything* for you."

She stared hard into my eyes. "I want you to kill Angel. I want you to kill him *tomorrow night*."

35.

re you okay?" Pepper narrowed her eyes at me, studying me.

"Yeah, I guess. Why?" I said.

"Aren't you supposed to be in study hall? Why are you
wandering around the halls?"

I blinked. I couldn't get her face to come into focus. The
long hallway stretched in front of me, gray lockers on both
sides, classroom doors closed because the bell had rung . . .
some kids on ladders hanging a maroon-and-gray banner
on the ceiling. . . . All a blur.

I'd felt confused all morning. Kind of in a daze.

Pepper stood with her hands on her waist, waiting for
an answer.

"I . . . don't know," I blurted out.

"You don't know what? You don't know why you're
wandering the halls?"

It was Pepper's first day back at school. She had the floppy
blue cap down tightly on her head. I knew she was afraid

kids would make fun of her if they saw her cut-up scalp. But, of course, she was wrong. Everyone was being super-nice to her. Everyone in school knew she'd been attacked, been through a horrible ordeal. No one would ever laugh about that.

Not even Diego, who liked to get in everyone's face and had a totally gross sense of humor. Diego drove Pepper to school this morning and told her she looked awesome in the cap. She said she thought maybe he'd been inhabited by a Martian or something. He didn't act like Diego at all.

"I'm just feeling a little weird," I told her. "Like my head is in a cloud. I think I froze my brain walking to school this morning."

Lizzy said she'd get a gun.

I said okay. Did I really say okay?

How COULD I?

She said she'd get me a gun, and I said okay.

I said I'd kill Angel tomorrow night.

I had a powerful urge to tell Pepper everything. I knew she would stop me. I knew she would take care of me. I knew Pepper would be . . . horrified.

I opened my mouth to start telling her about Lizzy in the snow this morning. But no sound came out. I made a choking sound.

Pepper stared harder at me. She grabbed my arm. "Michael? Do you need the nurse? You look so weird. Are you sick or something?"

Lizzy said she'd get me a gun.

She told me where to meet her.

"No. I'm okay. Really." I pointed to the door, the exit to the student parking lot. "Maybe a little fresh air . . ."

"It's still snowing, Michael. Don't go out without a coat."

I nodded. "Thanks, Mom."

"You're an idiot," she said.

I said I'd kill Angel tomorrow night.

"If I'm an idiot, why are you standing out in the hall, missing class and talking to me?"

She shrugged. "Beats me." She turned and started to walk away, adjusting the cap on her head. Her sneakers squeaked on the floor. She turned. "Are we still meeting after school to work on the yearbook?"

I nodded. "For sure."

She shook her head. "Don't wander the halls in a fog, Michael. Don't get weird, okay? We've got enough problems without you getting weird."

"Okay," I said. I watched her till she disappeared around a corner. I turned and jumped in surprise when I saw Mr. Oliphant, the principal, looming over me. He's about eight feet tall and big like a middle linebacker. In fact, I heard that he played linebacker in college at Howard University. The dark blue suits he always wears are always stretched at the shoulders and the chest.

Oliphant is the first black principal at Shadyside High, and everyone agrees he's an awesome guy. He's friendly, he always seems calm, he never loses it, and he's always out in the hall talking to kids.

"Didn't mean to sneak up on you, Michael," he said. The ceiling light spread over his glasses. I couldn't see his eyes. You expect a big guy like Oliphant to have a booming big-dude voice. But he's very soft-spoken and quiet.

"I . . . I should be in study hall," I blurted out.

Why did I say that? What's wrong with me?

"If you have a few minutes . . ." he said. He motioned with his head toward his office down the hall. "I'd like to talk to you about this girl I believe you encountered. Lizzy Walker?"

He put a big hand on my shoulder and gently began to lead me down the hall. "I understand we had an imposter in school, someone who didn't belong here."

"Lizzy said she'd get me a gun," I told him.

36.

He turned and squinted at me through his glasses. "What did you say?"

I swallowed. "I said I knew Lizzy. We kind of became friends . . . after I helped her find her way to a class. She always seemed to be lost."

Oliphant stepped into his office, nodding at Miss Greer, his secretary. "Come sit down, Michael. Let's talk about her. Did you have any clue at all that she wasn't registered here?"

"No. Not a clue," I said. "I didn't really get to know her that well."

Oliphant dropped into his leather desk chair. The seat cushion made a *whoosh* sound as he sat down. He really needed a bigger chair. He took off his glasses. His dark eyes studied me.

"Michael, you were here when this Lizzy Walker was assaulted in the school building," he said. "But you weren't an eyewitness—"

"No," I said. "I heard her scream. Then I came running into the hall and I . . . I found her on the floor."

He rubbed the bridge of his nose. "We are cooperating with the police investigation to find this young man they believe attacked her."

"His name is Angel," I said.

"So far, the police seem to be at a dead end. Not a clue as to where to find this man."

He waited for me to say something, but I didn't know what to say. It was an awkward silence. I stared at the photo of a little girl on his desk. Probably his daughter.

"I know the police believe this Walker girl can help them," Oliphant finally continued. "If you have any way of contacting her . . ."

I'm going to see her tomorrow night. She's going to help me kill Angel.

"I don't know where she is," I said. "She hasn't come back to school."

Oliphant tapped both hands on the desktop. "If you hear from her, or if you hear anything about her, let me know, okay?"

"Well, sure . . ."

"I'm sure I don't need to tell you this is very serious," he said. "We've had a trespasser in school for several days, and she was attacked by an intruder. A guy no one saw come or go. You can imagine that we're having serious talks about security issues here."

I stood up. "I'll keep my eyes open," I said. "If I see or hear anything . . ."

He nodded. "Thanks, Michael. You'd better get to class."

I started to the door, but he called me back. "I know you were good friends with Gabe," he said. "How are you doing? If you would like to talk to a counselor . . . ?"

"I-I think I'm okay," I stammered. "I think about him a lot. But I don't need to talk to anyone now."

He nodded, and I stepped out into the hall.

I'll feel a lot better after I kill Angel.

Diego stopped me after school. He stepped in front of me just as I closed my locker and bumped me hard with his belly. I went stumbling back and crashed into the wall.

"Hey, what's that about?" I cried.

"Just wanted to get your attention, Scout." He tugged me away from the wall. "Come with me. I've got a plan. For our *Macbeth* project."

"*Macbeth* project? We don't have a *Macbeth* project," I said. "Remember? We bagged our project because it sucked?"

"It's due tomorrow," he said. "I've got an awesome idea. You and me. We're going to nail it."

"I can't," I told him. "I told Pepper I'd meet her in the yearbook office. We have to look through a pile of dusty old yearbooks."

"That can wait," he said. "Follow me." He didn't give me

a choice. He gripped my shoulder and pushed me through the crowded hall.

"Why are you wearing that raincoat?" I asked. "What happened to your coat?"

"It's a costume," he said. "For *Macbeth*."

I narrowed my eyes at him. "Excuse me?"

He raised a small black leather case in his other hand. "I brought my GoPro camera," he said. "We're going to act out some scenes. Do some long speeches. Make it look really dark and scary. Miss Curdy will go nuts."

"I think *you're* nuts," I said.

"I'll do a scene and you'll do a scene," Diego said. "I'll take it home and put a background music track behind it tonight. We *can't* miss. But you've got to be serious. No goofing. No clowning around."

"Huh?" I cried. "*You're* telling *me* to be serious? That's a switch."

He turned me to the stairs. "Keep walking."

"Where are we going?" I demanded. "We can't stand out in the hall and act out scenes from *Macbeth*. We'll get a crowd. We'll look ridiculous."

We started down the stairs. "Not in the hall," Diego said. "In the basement. I found the perfect place."

The basement hall was dimly lit. Deserted. The door to the custodians' lounge was open. No one inside. We passed some supply closets and the textbook room. One large room was filled with electronic cables and wires, all tangled, reaching from the floor to the ceiling. So many wires

I couldn't see what they were attached to. At the far end, I could hear the loud hum of the furnace and boiler room.

"Yesterday, Miss Curdy sent me down to the book room to get some things for her," Diego explained. "She's always sending me for stuff because I'm big and strong and manly and everyone else is a wimp."

"If you don't say so yourself," I murmured.

He gave me a sharp push. "Anyway, when I was down here, I peeked into the furnace room, and it's perfect. It's dark and there are all these weird pipes in the ceiling and lots of steam and weird machines everywhere. It looks like it could be from a horror movie."

We were halfway down the hall, and I could already feel the heat pouring from the wide furnace room doorway. I heard a *chug chug chug* sound that must have been the boiler.

"I don't like this," I said. "Too hot in there."

"Man up," Diego said. "It won't take long. I brought the book. I'll read a scene, then you. Just stay back from the boiler."

"And you think Miss Curdy will be impressed?"

"No one else is doing a video," Diego said. "Check it out. How awesome is this?"

We stepped through the open doorway into the vast concrete room. It *did* look like the set for a horror movie. Wisps of steam floated from a back room. The boiler was solid black and looked like one of those pot-bellied stoves, only a hundred times as big. Beside it, the furnace was like a small house with dozens of fat pipes climbing out of the sides and top like octopus arms.

"Whoa! That boiler is burning hot!" I cried. I stepped to the other side of Diego, trying to move away from it.

"Just be careful," Diego said. "Stand over here. You can go first." He opened the GoPro case and pulled out the *Macbeth* play book. He handed it to me. Then he slid the little camera from the case.

"But this is crazy. I don't even know what I'm reading," I protested.

"Pick something," Diego said. "Here. Wear the raincoat." He tugged the long tan coat off. He wore a Shadyside High sweatshirt and baggy jeans under it. I took the raincoat from him. I knew it would be huge on me.

The boiler chugged behind us, sending off waves of heat. The furnace made a sighing sound, then came to life with a groan. The furnace shook. The whole room shook. Wisps of hot steam snaked low to the concrete floor.

"See? A horror movie," Diego said, grinning. "Atmosphere. Perfect for *Macbeth*."

"How do *you* know?" I demanded. "Have you read it?"

Diego grinned. "Not yet."

I started to skim through the play. I thought this was a totally dumb idea, but it was hard to argue with Diego. He seldom had any patience for anyone else's point of view. Can you picture a steamroller? That's Diego.

So I figured, *Let's just do this as fast as we can and get it over with.*

But then I had an idea. "There's a sword up in the art room," I told him.

He squinted at me. "Really?"

"Some kid made a sword out of wood and painted the blade silver. It would look great in our video. You know. A prop. Make us look professional."

Diego grinned at me. "I like it. Hurry. Go get it. I'll figure out the lighting and stuff while you're gone. I never really used this camera before."

I turned and headed back down the hall. I was happy to have an excuse to get out of the heat. The sound of the chugging boiler and roar of the furnace followed me all the way down the hall.

On the main floor, a few kids lingered outside the seniors' lounge, talking and laughing. Otherwise, the hall was empty. The building had been cleared out.

I was outside the art room, reaching for the door handle, when my phone dinged. A message. I fumbled the phone from my back pocket, raised the screen to my face and stared at the words:

If you can't stand the heat, stay out of the furnace.

It took me a few seconds to realize I was staring at a message from Angel. My brain whirred. It took a few more seconds to realize it wasn't a comment. It was a threat.

I wheeled around, lowered my head, and began to run full-speed back down the hall.

Diego, be okay, I prayed. *Please be okay. . . .*

37.

I heard his screams as soon as I reached the downstairs hall. His screams didn't sound human. Shrill and hoarse, they rang through the hall like the howls of an animal in pain.

The heat rolled over me as I burst into the furnace room, my shallow breaths wheezing noisily.

"Noooooooo!"

A horrified howl escaped my throat as my eyes stopped on Diego, strapped to the boiler.

A cord stretched tight around his chest held his back to the churning boiler. Diego thrashed his arms helplessly, eyes shut, mouth open in scream after anguished scream. "Help me! Hellllp me! It's . . . so . . . hot . . . Oh, please . . . I can't . . . I can't . . . I'm burning . . . I'm BURNING!"

His face, darkened to a deep red, was drenched in sweat. As he twisted his head, struggling to pull away from the intense heat, I could see blisters already breaking open on the back of his neck.

Wave after wave of heat roared off the boiler. Diego let out one more animal scream. Then his head slumped forward. His arms fell limply to his sides. He didn't move.

He'll burn to death.

Is he already dead?

The horrifying questions swam in my head as I fought back my shock and terror and lurched forward. The heat radiating off the boiler made my face burn. My eyes began to water. I struggled to breathe.

Grabbing the cord in both trembling hands, I fumbled till I found the knot on the other side of the boiler. I couldn't see at all through my tearing eyes. My whole body felt on fire, as if I was roasting on a spit.

Frantically, I struggled with the knot. Loosened it. Yes. Loosened it and kept working at it . . . until the cord snapped off and slid to the floor.

Diego's head bobbed forward, and he slumped lifelessly into my arms. I caught him. Staggering back under his weight, I gave a hard tug to pull him from the boiler.

A deafening *rrrrrippppp* made me gasp. The sound of Velcro tearing open. A sound I knew I'd never forget.

I raised my gaze, forced my eyes to the boiler—and opened my mouth in a silent howl of horror and disgust.

Diego's sweatshirt had stuck to the metal boiler. The fabric melted against the intense heat. And his skin . . . oh, wow . . . the skin . . . the skin of Diego's back—*it stuck to the boiler wall.*

"*Nooooo! Oh, nooooo!*" Horrified howls escaped my throat.

When I pulled him off the boiler . . . I ripped his skin off . . . left his skin sizzling on the metal boiler wall. And as I lowered Diego face down on the floor, I couldn't avert my eyes in time . . . and I saw bubbling rivulets of blood . . . bits of shirt fabric . . .

His back . . . his back was nothing but raw red meat.

38.

Police swarmed the school. Pistols drawn, dark-uniformed cops made their way down the halls, moving cautiously, stopping to inspect every classroom. I imagined that Angel was far from the school by now.

I phoned my parents and told them to hurry over. My hands shook so hard, I could barely hold the phone. As I spoke to my dad, I heard the ambulance siren as they took Diego away.

"He's breathing," someone said from the crowd of on-lookers. "He's still alive."

I could still feel the heat of the boiler on my skin. Every time I closed my eyes, I saw the shiny raw meat of Diego's back, pulsing with dark blood. And I couldn't erase from my memory the sound of his skin ripping away.

Meat. His back was raw meat, shiny and wet, the blood pouring down over the red meat like steak sauce.

Outside the windows, I saw the late afternoon sun lowering behind the bare winter trees. The police were still searching the school, every floor, every classroom, every inch of the basement and furnace room.

Did they find anything helpful? They wouldn't tell me.

I felt sick, too sick to talk to them. But what choice did I have? I was the only witness, the only one who could tell the story.

When I finished telling them everything I knew, everything I'd seen, I couldn't believe they said to carry on as normal. "We're closing in on him," they said.

Were they lying?

They told the principal to keep the school open. They said they'd increase their patrol. They said school life should go on. But how could it?

As my parents drove me home, I couldn't speak. In a strange way, I blamed myself.

If only I hadn't waited to kill Angel.

Now I knew I was ready. I knew I could do it. I knew I could kill him tomorrow night. No problem.

Act normal? Nothing seemed normal at school the next day, especially with cops stationed at every doorway.

Oliphant held an assembly to talk about what had happened to Diego. That didn't seem normal, either. He talked a lot about safety in numbers. I didn't really listen. I couldn't tell you anything he said. I don't think anyone else could, either.

You could feel the fear in the auditorium, feel the tension in the unusual hushed silence.

Act normal. How stupid was that?

After school, I found Pepper in the yearbook office, standing behind a tall stack of old Shadyside High yearbooks. I tossed my backpack on the floor and stepped up to the table.

"Here we are, acting normal," she said. "Just like Oliphant told us to."

I sighed. "Do you think we'll ever feel normal again?"

Pepper shrugged. "What do you hear about Diego? Did you hear anything from the hospital?"

"Critical but stable," I said.

She tugged at the sides of her floppy blue cap. "What does that *mean*?"

I shook my head. "I don't know. But that's what the doctors keep saying. I guess the stable part is good."

She put her hand on the back of my hand. "Michael, you look so pale."

"I can't stop thinking about . . ." I didn't finish the sentence.

"Let's change the subject," she said. "You know. Act normal. Let's talk about me."

"Whatever," I murmured.

"Know what I hate?" she said.

"What?"

"I hate everyone telling me how great I look in this cap all day long. *Oh, Pepper, it's awesome. Oh, Pepper, where did you get it? Oh, I love it.* It's like, is everyone I know a total fake?"

"They're just trying to be nice," I said. "You *do* look kind of cute in it."

"Shut up."

"People try to be nice and it makes you angry?" I said.

"Everything makes me angry," she muttered. She slammed her fist on a yearbook, sending up a wave of dust. "They're not being nice. They're saying they're so glad I wore the cap so they don't have to look at a bald-headed freak."

"Not true," I said. "You know, your hair will grow back."

She remained silent for a long while, her eyes out the window. Finally, she turned back to me. "After all that's gone down, are you still daydreaming about Lizzy Walker?"

"Haven't seen her," I lied. "Are we going to go through these old yearbooks, or what? I really don't feel like it, but maybe it'll take our minds off . . . everything."

"Okay. We'll look at yearbooks. Here. I brought you a present," Pepper said. She handed me a small package.

"Tissues?"

"Well, the last time we tried to look at these old books, you started sneezing your head off. So . . ."

"Thanks," I said, tossing the tissue pack onto the table. "Where shall we start?"

She lifted a yearbook off the pile and lowered it to the table between us. "Why not start with this one? 1950."

"Wow. Almost seventy years ago," I said.

"Duh. So you can count."

I frowned at her." Pepper, you're not cheering me up."

"Sorry."

She lifted the old yearbook cover and opened the book to a page near the middle. The book smelled sour, kind of musty, like a closet in the attic. She pointed to a page of photos. "Prom 1950," she read. "The theme is *The Wizard of Oz*." She snickered. "Look at these kids. The girls all have such short hair. Wow. Check out those long skirts. Like Granny wears."

"We should put some of these photos on the blog," I said. "They're a riot."

Pepper turned to the senior photos near the back. The faces from seventy years ago stared up at us. "They were our age but they look so much older," she said.

"That's because the boys are all wearing jackets and ties," I said.

"And the girls are all wearing those frilly white blouses with little collars. Totally weird. And look. They all have a single strand of pearls around their necks."

I laughed. "Do you think they all used the same pearls? Passed them to each other for their yearbook photo?"

"Wow. This girl is wearing a black sweater, really tight. And look at that dark lipstick. She must have been weird."

"Check out this guy with the bow tie and all the pimples. Bet he was real popular."

I turned the page. "Think kids will laugh at our photos and call us freaks seventy years from now?" Pepper asked.

I didn't answer. I was staring hard at a photo near the

top of the page. "Uh . . . Pepper," I said. I poked my finger on the photo. "Look at this one."

She pushed my finger away. She gazed at it. Blinked a few times. Lowered her face to the page. "I don't believe it," she muttered. "That girl . . ."

"She looks exactly like Lizzy Walker," I said.

39.

"That's crazy," Pepper said. She picked up the yearbook and brought it close to her face. "She doesn't just *look* like Lizzy. She's Lizzy in every way."

I grabbed the book. "Come on. Let me see it, too." I studied the photo. "Same black hair. Same big dark eyes. Same serious expression. Maybe it's Lizzy's mother."

"Seventy years ago?" Pepper said. "Lizzy's mother can't be that old."

My finger moved over the caption beneath. "It says her name is Beth Palmieri." I turned to Pepper. "Why does that name sound familiar?"

"Beats me," she said. "Beth Palmieri. Doesn't sound familiar to *me*."

I stared at the dark eyes, at the somber expression of the girl in the photo. No one else could look that much like Lizzy. But this photo was taken seventy years ago. . . .

"Beth . . . Beth . . ." Pepper murmured the name. She tugged at my arm. Her expression turned thoughtful. "You know . . . Beth and Lizzy . . . they're both parts of the same name."

"Huh? What do you mean?" I didn't make the connection.

"They're both parts of the name Elizabeth. They're both nicknames for Elizabeth. Lizzy and Beth."

I nodded, my eyes on the photo. "True. But so what?"

And suddenly I had a flash of memory. The graveyard. The tombstones we were rubbing for Miss Beach's class. Lizzy standing so sadly in front of the twin tombstones on the low hill . . .

"I just remembered something," I told Pepper.

"Like what?"

"Like a gravestone rubbing that Lizzy wanted to make. Remember that weird foggy day in the graveyard?"

"What about it?" Pepper said.

"Did you drive this morning?"

She nodded.

"Let's go," I said. "To the old cemetery. I'm pretty sure I'm right."

Pepper glanced out the window. "Michael, it's getting dark out. It looks like it's getting ready to snow again. I really don't feel like going to the cemetery."

"Come on," I said. I put both hands on her back and gave her a push toward the door. "We have a mystery to solve."

Pepper parked near the gate, and we made our way through drifts of snow to the cemetery entrance. The sky was a charcoal gray, storm clouds hanging low overhead. A steady wind howled through the old trees, making the limbs creak and shake.

"Like an old-time horror movie," I murmured, glancing around. A shiver ran down my back. I tightened my hood around my head.

Pepper narrowed her eyes at me. "Why are we here, Michael? It wouldn't kill you to explain."

I tugged her hood over her face with both hands. "I'll show you. Follow me."

The snow was deep here. No one had cleared a path through the rows of graves. The wind suddenly stopped, and an eerie hush fell over us. The only sounds were our boots on the snow and my panting breaths.

"The silence is creepy," I said, taking Pepper's hand and turning toward the low hill.

"Shut up, Michael. Are you trying to scare me?"

I suddenly pictured the waves of fog that day our class was here. Billowing fog rising from the ground and the shadowy blur, the form of Angel climbing up from that tall gravestone, standing so still, like a mirage in the thick gray mist, standing still but watching . . . watching me . . . a silent, cold threat.

I shivered again.

Pepper gave me a push that sent me stumbling over a tall icy snowdrift. "Why are we here? Tell me."

"This is why," I said. I led her up to the two granite stones, side by side, tilting a little toward each other. We both gazed at the inscriptions. "Yes. I'm right," I said.

Pepper read the names and dates out loud. "Angelo Palmieri. 1912 to 1950. Beth Palmieri. 1934 to 1950." She turned to me, her eyes wide. "Michael, this is her grave. She died the same year the yearbook came out. Her senior year."

"This is the gravestone Lizzy wanted to rub that day," I said. "She said it was a father and daughter. When I walked up to her, she was just staring at the girl's stone, not moving, this weird sad expression on her face."

"So . . . Beth Palmieri must have been someone in Lizzy's family," Pepper said. "Her grandmother maybe? Someone Lizzy was named after."

I gazed at the engraved words on the tombstone as the wind picked up again, howling its eerie song. "Someone," I said, "who was Lizzy's identical twin."

Pepper took a step back. She tugged her hood down. "Michael, we've got to get home. It's late."

I nodded and started to follow her to the gate.

"Do you want to get together tonight?" she asked. "Study for the Government exam?"

Lizzy is getting a gun.

"No, I can't," I said. "I'm busy."

40.

At dinner, I tried to answer Mom and Dad's questions about my day and join in their conversation. Everyone avoided what was really on our minds—Angel, Diego, and all the horrors. My parents began talking about a spring vacation as soon as my graduation was over. Should we do a beach vacation, or should we go on a road trip somewhere interesting?

Normally, I love discussions about vacations. But tonight I was distracted and fuzzy, I mean like I had clouds in my brain, and I know my parents could see there was something going on with me. They kept looking at me and asking if I felt okay. That's a pretty good sign they knew something was up.

And yes, something was *definitely* up.

"Guess what, Mom and Dad? I'm going to meet Lizzy tonight in the Fear Street Woods, and I'm going to shoot Angel."

Those words flashed through my mind. The truth. But, of course, I couldn't say them. I couldn't tell my parents what was up. And I definitely couldn't tell them why I was doing it, why I couldn't say no, why I couldn't come to my senses and realize that I was about to do something insane.

I'm sure Lizzy didn't hypnotize me. But I felt under a spell. I knew I had no choice, no will of my own. I was going to do this thing. I couldn't stop myself.

I'm doing it for Gabe and Diego, I told myself. *Angel killed my best friend. And maybe he killed Diego, too. I need to pay him back.*

I waited half an hour after my parents went to bed. Luckily, they are sound sleepers. Then I took Mom's car keys from the bowl in the front hall and crept out the door.

As I zipped my parka, a chill rolled down my back. It was a cold night, a freezing drizzle raining down from a solid purple sky. The snow had formed a hard layer on top, and I slipped twice making my way to the car at the curb.

Mom had replaced the totaled car with a little Honda. I had only driven it once, and it took me awhile to fumble the key into the ignition.

The little car still had that new-car smell. Normally, I love that fresh aroma. But tonight, it only meant that I was heading into new territory. Nothing seemed familiar, not the car, not even Park Drive, which I have ridden up and down for most of my life.

The snow had been cleared, and the few cars that were out moved easily. I followed Park Drive all the way to Fear

Street and made a right, heading to the woods. The houses on Fear Street all stood far back from the road, usually on top of sloping hills covered in trees and shrubs. Many houses were hidden behind tall hedges.

Some of the houses were enormous, like castles. Everyone in Shadyside knew about the Fear Mansion, which was owned by the weird family the street was named after. The mansion burned to the ground during a huge party the Fears had thrown. For some reason, the party guests couldn't escape and were all burned to a crisp. Dozens of them, screaming while flames poured over them, danced over them, charred their skin and then melted their bones, till only ashes remained. And still the screams rose from the ashes.

At least, that's the story I heard from a teacher at school. The story has been told so many times over the years, I think everyone tells it differently. But the blackened remains of the house remained for decades, a reminder to all who passed by it of the evil that family supposedly brought to the street and the woods behind it.

The ruins of the mansion were finally cleared away. Before I was born, I think. But nothing new has been built on the huge grounds. It's just a big, empty lot. Sometimes in the summer, kids gather there late at night and party. Like it's a park or something.

Tonight, the Fear yard lay dark and empty. As I drove past, my headlights washed over some creatures near the street. A family of raccoons, five or six of them, trudged in a straight line over the snow, heads down, making their way to the woods.

The car slid as I pulled to the curb near where the trees began. Not another car on the street. I killed the headlights and sat there for a while, gazing out at the night, my heart racing in my chest, my breaths fast and shallow.

The windshield immediately began to steam up. A full moon slid out from the low, heavy clouds, and the trees appeared to light up, as if a spotlight had been shining on them.

Nothing looked real to me. Under the moonlight, it all looked too silvery to be real. I could suddenly see so clearly, the outline of each tree, all winter bare, and the low wall of shrubs and weeds that lined the shimmering ground.

Unreal.

I pushed open the car door and climbed out. I gasped in shock as the cold air rushed to greet me. The woods smelled like pine. The drizzle had stopped, and the air was perfectly still. The trees didn't sway or bend. Nothing moved.

As if the woods were dead.

As I started to cross the snow toward the trees, the moon slid behind the clouds. I watched the inky black shadow spread over the ground like a dark blanket, covering the trees, then the snow in front of me, then over me.

After our long kiss, Lizzy had whispered instructions in my ear. Now, I had a moment of panic when I couldn't find the path Lizzy had described that morning. The path led to the clearing where Lizzy said she'd be waiting. I knew if I didn't find it, I could be wandering around in here all night.

You won't wander all night. You'll freeze to death before morning.

I turned and strode to the left. And squinted at a solid wall of birch trees. I realized I'd gone too far. I swung back and started to the right. I pulled out my phone and turned it into a flashlight. It wasn't very bright. The light didn't go far. But I found the path, a narrow opening between two fat trees, and ducking my head against their low limbs, edged into the deeper darkness of the woods.

I took a few steps—and a strong hand grabbed me from behind. Tightened around my shoulder and swung me off-balance.

I turned and uttered a cry of surprise.

"Pepper? What are *you* doing here?"

41.

She had the hood of her parka pulled tight over her head. In the light from my phone, I saw her eyes accusing me, questioning me. She held onto my arm with one gloved hand.

"I saw you leave your house, Michael," she said, her voice hollow, muffled by the trees and the still, dead air. "I was coming over to borrow your Government notes. Didn't you get my text?"

"N-no," I stammered.

"I saw you sneak out. I followed you here," Pepper said. "What's going on? What are you doing here?"

"I . . . can't explain," I said. I kept the light on her face. "Pepper, you have to go. You shouldn't be here."

She narrowed her eyes at me. "I'm not leaving till you tell me what you're doing in the Fear Street Woods in the middle of the night." She grabbed my arm again. "Michael, I found you wandering the halls at school yesterday afternoon.

You've been through a terrible thing with Diego. I know. I know you're upset. But . . . tell me. What is it? What's up with you?"

I gazed at her in the quivering white light from the phone. "Pepper, please go home," I said. "Please listen to me. Just leave, okay?"

"No way, Michael. I—"

A voice from the trees interrupted us. "Michael? I see you. Over here."

"Lizzy!" I called. I turned and started toward the voice.

Pepper hurried behind me. "Lizzy is here? What is *she* doing here?"

"Please leave," I repeated.

"This way, Michael," Lizzy called. I squinted down the path. I could hear her but I couldn't see her.

"This can't be happening," Pepper said, bumping me from behind.

Lizzy came into view, waving both arms, signaling me toward her. Her hood was down. Her dark hair flowed behind her. I tucked my phone into my jeans pocket. I didn't need its light anymore.

My chest was heaving, my rapid breaths puffing up clouds in front of me. "Lizzy . . ." I uttered, my voice a hoarse whisper.

She stood in a small clearing in front of a tight clump of trees. Her face twisted in surprise when she saw Pepper beside me. "What is *she* doing here?"

Pepper bumped me aside and strode up to Lizzy, her eyes

narrowed angrily, her fists clenched. "What are *you* doing here, Lizzy?" Pepper demanded. "What is this about? Why should Michael meet you here?"

"You weren't invited," Lizzy said softly, in a voice just above a whisper. "You weren't invited, Pepper, so just go, okay? Turn around and go away."

Pepper didn't move. I saw her eyes go wide. I saw her expression turn from surprise to anger. She uttered a sharp cry—and dove at Lizzy like an attacking tiger.

Lizzy raised one gloved hand in the air. She moved it in a tight circle.

And Pepper froze. Her eyes locked in a wide-eyed stare. Her mouth hung open. One fist hovered in the air. Pepper froze in place. I mean, like a statue.

Lizzy made another circle with her hand. A smile spread over her face, a pleased smile.

I stared in shock at Pepper, frozen in front of me, frozen as if someone had hit a Pause button. She didn't blink. She didn't seem to be breathing.

It took me awhile to get over my shock. Finally, I stepped up to Pepper and grabbed her by the shoulders. "Are you okay? Can you hear me?"

Her eyes stared blankly ahead.

I shook her. "Can you hear me? Can you?"

She gave no sign.

I spun around to Lizzy, my heart throbbing in my chest, the blood pulsing at my temples. A wave of dizziness swept over me, and I struggled to fight it off.

"How did you do that?" I cried. "What did you do to her? How? How can you freeze someone like that?"

The smile didn't fade from her face. Her dark eyes shimmered in the dim light that filtered down through the trees. "I know a few little tricks," she said. "People shouldn't mess with me, Michael."

"Did you kill her?" I demanded, my voice breaking. "Can you bring her back? Unfreeze her?"

She laughed, a cold laugh, sharp like the tinkle of cut glass.

"Answer me!" I cried.

"Forget about Pepper, Michael," Lizzy said. "You've got bigger worries than Pepper."

My mind was spinning. "You hypnotized me or something, didn't you!" I cried. "You cast some kind of spell on me? Like what you just did to Pepper? Is that why I had to come here tonight?"

"So many questions," she said. "I asked you to kill Angel, remember? And you agreed."

"I agreed because you did something to me. You have powers. You—"

"Don't try to figure it out, Michael," she said. "I think it will all become clear . . . very soon."

"Why are we here?" I repeated. "Tell me, Lizzy. Where is Angel? What is this about?"

She made a pouty face, sticking out her lips. "I'm afraid I lied a little," she said in a whisper.

"Lied? What do you mean?" I cried.

"Yes, I lied. Sorry about that. Especially since we're bloods." Her eyes flashed with sudden excitement. "But, Michael, the truth is, we're not here to kill Angel. Angel and I are going to kill *you*."

crazy! --

42.

My mouth dropped open. I uttered a startled cry. For a moment I felt paralyzed, frozen in place like Pepper beside me.

Run, I told myself. *Turn around and run.*

But I couldn't leave Pepper. And if I tried to run, Lizzy would probably raise her hand and freeze me, too.

My thoughts were a jumble of fear and disbelief. I stared at Lizzy's excited face, struggling to understand what was happening here.

Before I could move, Angel stepped out from the trees. His head was bare, his stringy black hair hanging down over the sides of his face. He wore the same long, black overcoat I'd always seen him in. His boots crunched over the snow. He stepped up beside Lizzy, his eyes locked on me, his expression sour, threatening.

"I-I . . . don't understand," I stammered, my voice high and shrill. "Tell me what this is about. Why are you doing this?"

Lizzy linked her arm in Angel's. He kept his eyes trained on me.

The moon appeared again, its pale light making Angel's face silvery white. *Like a ghost,* I thought. They both appeared to fade in the moonlight, their skin papery and pale.

"Poor guy. You're so confused," Lizzy said, sneering the words. "Let me give you a hint." She squeezed Angel's arm and leaned her cheek against the shoulder of his overcoat.

"Tell me," I demanded.

"For one thing, his name isn't Angel," she said. "I made that name up. His name is Aaron. Aaron Dooley. Does that give you a clue, Michael?"

Aaron Dooley?

"No," I said. "No, it doesn't."

Lizzy tossed her head back and sneered again. Her dark eyes flashed with anger. "You and Aaron are related, Michael."

"Stop teasing me!" I cried. "Just tell me—"

"Aaron is Martin Dooley's nephew," Lizzy said, squeezing his arm again.

That name clicked in. I felt my heart skip a beat. "Martin Dooley?" I cried. "My grandfather? Th-that's crazy. Grandpa Dooley died years ago and—"

"Shut up and listen," Aaron spoke up for the first time. Lizzy had hold of his right arm. He clenched the fist on this left and raised it menacingly.

Lizzy narrowed her eyes at me. She took a step toward

me. "Your Grandpa Dooley murdered my father," she said. "He murdered my father in 1950."

"You're crazy," I said. "That was almost seventy years ago. You couldn't have been alive in 1950. My grandpa never murdered anyone. He—"

"Shut up! Shut up!" Aaron screamed. His eyes went wide with fury. His whole body tensed, preparing to attack me.

"Listen, Michael." Lizzy's voice cracked with emotion. Her eyes burned into mine. "Your grandfather had my father torn to pieces. I was there. I watched. Your grandfather owned a stable. He starved his horses so they would be hungry enough to devour my father. They tore him apart, Michael. Do you understand? Tore him apart and ate him while I watched and listened to his screams."

My mouth hung open. I struggled to make sense of this. I shook my head hard as if trying to clear it. "No," I said softly. "Grandpa Dooley was a quiet man. He was nearly blind. He had some kind of accident when he was young. It burned his face and he lost one eye."

"He wanted to murder me, too," Lizzy continued, ignoring me. Her face shone in the moonlight, the anger making her chin tremble. "But I ran. I don't know how I found the strength, but I ran."

"Lizzy, this is impossible. Why are you making up this story? Are you totally crazy?" The words blurted from my mouth. I regretted them instantly.

Aaron roared forward and grabbed me by the shoulders.

He spun me around roughly and wrapped a strong arm around my chest. He held me in place and pushed his fist into my back.

I struggled to free myself, but he was surprisingly strong.

"Let go of me!" I screamed. "You're crazy. You're both crazy!"

Lizzy raised a hand. I gasped, thinking she was going to freeze me. But she only wanted to silence me. "Let me show you where I ran, Michael. Let me show you how I escaped from your grandfather's men."

Aaron gave me a hard push. I stumbled and started to fall. He caught me, stood me up, and gave me another hard shove.

"Where are you taking me?" I cried. "Where are we going?"

"You'll see," Lizzy said, leading the way. "You're not going to live happily ever after, Michael. You're never coming out of the woods."

43.

They forced me through the line of birch trees, then past it. The moonlight washed down on us through the bare tree limbs overhead, casting dim shadows on the snow. The wind had blown the snow into low hills and valleys. Some of the drifts were high enough to cover the shrubs that lined the path. It made them look like cartoon ghosts.

Aaron had my arms pinned at my sides. He kept shoving me forward, showing me he was in charge.

In my panic, Lizzy's story kept repeating in my mind. She had to be crazy. The story couldn't be true. But how, I wondered, did it get in her head? She couldn't really believe that she was alive in 1950. And, what would make her think that my poor half-blind grandpa Dooley had murdered her father?

After we passed through another clump of trees, Aaron gave me a hard shove that made me cry out. And I gazed at the black opening of a cave. It looked like a dark, open mouth cut into a mound of stone.

"Here we are," Lizzy said. "This is where I ran that night, Michael." She motioned to the cave opening.

"I-I . . . don't understand," I stammered.

Aaron gave me a hard shove in the back that sent me sprawling against the snowy side of the cave. "Just shut up and listen."

"This is how I escaped," Lizzy said. "You won't believe it, but it's true. I'm not insane. I'm not delusional. Every word I'm telling you is true."

I brushed snow off the front of my coat. I opened my mouth to say something, but thought better of it. Behind me, Aaron was ready to give me another shove.

"The cave you are staring into is a time tunnel," Lizzy said, her eyes burning into mine. "It's a direct connection between the past and today."

"Sorry," I said. "I'm not into science fiction."

"Neither am I," Lizzy snapped. "But what I'm telling you is true. I ran into this cave the night my father was murdered. It pulled me in and shoved me through time, and I ended up here, far in the future."

She stepped up to me. Her breath steamed against my face. "Do you know how frightened I was, Michael? Here I was, still sixteen, but over seventy years in the future. Here I was, and I had nothing. Do you know why I had to steal food from that market?"

She sneered at me. "Yes, I know you saw me. I had to

steal that food because I had nothing. No money. Nothing at all. Do you understand what I'm telling you?"

"Not really," I said. "You don't seriously expect me to believe this, do you?"

Her eyes flared angrily. "I'm telling you the truth," she said through gritted teeth. "Here I was, far in the future, and I had nothing." The wind rustled her hood. She pushed it down and let her hair fall free.

"Well, actually, I *did* have one thing," she continued. "I had my need, Michael."

I squinted at her. "Your need?"

"My need for revenge. My need to avenge my father's death. To pay back Martin Dooley for destroying my family. That's what I had. Something burning in my chest . . . burning all the time. . . . The need to make Martin Dooley pay."

"But my grandfather—" I started.

"Shut up!" Aaron gave me a hard slap that sent my head spinning. The sound echoed all around. The pain made me shut my eyes. "I warned you," he said, both fists still curled.

"But your grandfather died in 1985," Lizzy continued. "Is that what you wanted to tell me, Michael? Yes. Martin Dooley was long gone when I arrived here. Too late. I was too late. Isn't that sad?"

I didn't reply. I was still trying to rub the pain from my face. I gazed around the dark woods. If I had to make a run for it, which way should I run?

"So you see, Michael, I had no choice," Lizzy said. "I

couldn't pay back Martin Dooley. But I *could* pay back his grandson. You. I could make you and everyone close to you pay for what he did."

"You're crazy!" I shouted. "You're totally nuts!"

Aaron grabbed my arm. I ducked my head to avoid another slap. "Do you hear yourself? Do you hear how insane that story is?" I shouted.

She clenched her jaw. "It's . . . all . . . true," she said, pronouncing one word at a time. "All . . . true."

In my panic, I'd forgotten about the old yearbook photo Pepper and I had found. The photo from 1950 with the girl who looked just like Lizzy. *No. Oh, no,* I thought. *Her crazy time-travel story is true.*

"Are you Beth Palmieri?" I blurted out.

She nodded. "That's my name."

Beth Palmieri from 1950. And her gravestone is in the old cemetery.

"But . . . you're dead!" I screamed. "We saw your tombstone. They buried you. You're dead."

She shook her head. "They never found me. They must have assumed I died like my father. They must have buried an empty casket."

She brought her face close to mine. "I'm alive. I'm alive and sixteen. Didn't you think I was alive when you kissed me?"

"Yes," I said. "But . . ."

"I'm alive and sixteen, thanks to this time tunnel." She motioned to the cave. "But do you want to hear something sad? You can only go into the cave once. You can only take it in one direction. I'm stuck here, Michael. Stuck nearly seventy years in the future. I can't go back. But there's one thing that is making me happy. Having my revenge. Hurting you and your friends."

She kissed my cheek. It wasn't an affectionate kiss. It was an angry kiss. A spiteful kiss. She kissed me, then licked my cheek.

It sent a shiver down my whole body. The coldest kiss anyone ever got.

"I'm not an evil person," she said. "But after seeing what your grandfather did to my father, I have no choice. Do you understand? Do you understand why you have to die?"

"No," I said. I squeezed my hands against the sides of my throbbing head. "No. This is too much. This is too crazy. You—you're Beth Palmieri, and you went to Shady-side High in 1950. . . . And you're like a witch or something?"

She nodded, her dark eyes suddenly dull and dead. "My grandmother taught me some little tricks."

"What are you going to do to Pepper?" I demanded. "Are you just going to leave her like that?"

"That's so cute that you worry about her when *you* are the one in so much trouble," Lizzy replied. "Don't worry. The spell will wear off. Maybe it will wear off before she freezes to death."

"Can we hurry this up?" Aaron interrupted. "It's cold, you know?"

I spun around. "And who is this guy? Angel or Aaron, or whatever you want to call him. Does he come from the past, too? Like maybe caveman days?"

"Not funny," he said. "You're in a world of trouble, buddy. Why make jokes?"

"I explained that you and Aaron are related, Michael. Aren't you pleased to meet your great-uncle?"

"No. I hate him," I said. "I hate him for what he did to my friends."

"I hated Aaron, too," Lizzy said. She smiled at Aaron. "I hated him with all my heart. I thought Aaron was a loathsome creep. I saw him. . . . He watched my father die. Aaron stood there and watched my father suffer and die."

Aaron took a step toward Lizzy. She motioned for him to stay close to me.

Maybe she could read my mind. Maybe she knew I was looking for the best way to run, to escape from these two lunatics.

"That night, I didn't realize the truth," she continued. "That Aaron was too horrified to move, that he was too sickened by what he saw . . . so sick and frightened by what they did to my father, he was paralyzed."

A gust of cold wind fluttered her hair. Her eyes remained on Aaron. "Then Martin Dooley's men spotted me. I turned and ran, ran for my life. They wanted to kill me, too, the only witness to their horrible crime. Aaron came chasing after me. I thought he wanted to capture me and drag me back to them.

"I had no reason to trust him," she continued. "We . . . we had a bad time. . . . A bad moment a few days before. I actually hated him. But I was wrong about him. Aaron loved me. He loved me so much, he followed me into the cave. He followed me to another time. And he's been helping me ever since we arrived here. Helping me get my revenge. We planned it all. The snowmobile accident. Everything."

I narrowed my eyes at her. "You used your powers? You *forced* me to crash my snowmobile into him?"

Lizzy tossed back her head and laughed that cold, tinkling laugh. "You catch on quickly."

"Enough explaining," Aaron chimed in. "Save it for the movies. I'm freezing here. Let's finish this guy. Mission accomplished."

I didn't give Lizzy a chance to answer. I took a deep breath, swung around and, bending low, charged forward— and butted my head as hard as I could into the pit of Aaron's stomach.

44.

*H*e opened his mouth in a startled grunt, bent in two, and went down hard. He sat in the snow, hands pressed against his gut.

I whirled away from him and took off running. My shoes slapped the crusty snow as I picked up speed. I leaned into the wind, ran low like a running back, my heaving breaths noisy, heart booming.

I'd run several yards when I stumbled over a fallen tree limb hidden beneath the snow. I fell hard onto my stomach. My breath burst out in a painful *whoosh.* Gasping for breath, my chest aching, I tried to push myself to my feet.

But Aaron landed on my back with both knees.

"Smooth move, ace," he said.

I groaned. My face sank into the snow. He grabbed the back of my head and held it under the surface. Held it . . . pressed it down with all his strength. . . . Held me down until I felt my lungs about to burst. I opened my mouth, struggling to breathe, and got a choking mouthful of muddy, icy snow.

Finally, Aaron wrapped his fingers in my hair and tugged my head up. I choked in breath after breath, my chest throbbing. He pulled me up roughly, gave me a hard shove, and forced me back to Lizzy.

She stood in a beam of silvery moonlight with her arms crossed in front of her parka, eyes on me as Aaron dragged me back, her expression cold now, angry. "Cave time, Michael," she said softly.

My face felt frozen from being under the snow. My whole body shivered. "You . . . you're both crazy," I shouted. "You can't really expect me to believe you came from seventy years ago. You need a doctor. You're both *sick*!"

"Well, you'll find out if we're telling the truth or not," Lizzy said. "You're going into the cave now. You're going back in time."

Aaron grabbed me from behind and pulled my hands behind my back. "Too bad you won't be able to give us a report on how you like it," he rasped in my ear. "It's a one-way trip. You can only go in the cave once."

"Aren't you excited, Michael?" Lizzy said, stepping closer. "Aren't you excited to visit a time in the past?"

I didn't reply. I tried to tug my arms free, but Aaron held on tightly and shoved me forward.

"Only one small problem," Lizzy said, eyes flashing merrily. "If you travel back too far, you might land in a time before you were born. So it probably means you won't exist." She tsk-tsked. "No more Michael Frost. No more Martin Dooley's grandson. So sad. But, come on, Michael. Aren't you going to say goodbye? Do you want a goodbye kiss? I know you enjoyed my kisses so much."

I stared into the darkness beyond the mouth of the cave.

"It's just a cave," I said. "Go ahead. Push me in. Big whoop. Big surprise when I'm still here. And you're both still crazy."

But then I heard a hollow rush of air inside the cave, like the sound a seashell makes when you hold it to your ear. And then I thought I heard voices . . . distant muffled voices . . . a jumble of voices all talking at once from deep inside the cave . . . voices carried on the steady whisper of wind.

Voices from the past?

"Whoa." My heart skipped a beat. Suddenly, I believed.

Suddenly, I knew that Lizzy and Aaron were telling the truth. The cave was a time tunnel. They came from 1950. That Shadyside High yearbook photo of Lizzy in 1950 was proof. What more proof did I need?

It was all true. And now I was staring at a time-travel adventure of my own. One that would be very short. A trip into the past from which I could never return.

I believed it now. I knew it was true. It was happening.

My head throbbed. Panic sent chill after chill down my body.

Lizzy stepped up beside me and grabbed one arm. Aaron

held onto the other. They forced me forward. The cave opening appeared to grow as I moved toward it, like a huge mouth silently sliding open.

"No. Please—" I choked out. "Please."

They pushed me into the blackness of the cave. The rush of wind grew louder in my ears. The voices, so far away, so faint, dozens of them talking at once . . . the voices from deep in the darkness.

I tried to push back. But the two of them held me tight. Moved me forward. Forced me into the deep, deep well of blackness.

I'm fading, I thought. *I feel so weak.*

Here I go. Vanishing. I'm vanishing now.

Here I go.

45.

The cold darkness rolled over me like an ocean wave. Lizzy and Aaron held onto my arms. But I could barely feel them now. Standing at the cave opening, I knew I was fading into the rush of wind, the deep inky darkness.

The time tunnel was pulling me now. I felt a strange force, a powerful tug, pulling me into the cave. I was gone . . . gone.

And then a high shrill siren scream broke the spell.

A scream from somewhere far behind me. Staring into the blackness, I recognized it. Pepper's scream from back in the clearing.

The scream must have startled Lizzy and Aaron, too. They took a stuttering step back. Let go of me. Let go for a second.

I didn't hesitate. I knew I had two seconds to act. Alert because of the scream, I summoned my strength.

I lowered my hands behind them—and *shoved* Lizzy and

Aaron with all my might. Shoved them into the cave. And watched them stumble forward.

It happened too fast for them to cry out.

Lizzy fell to her knees on the dirt cave floor. Aaron struggled to regain his balance.

Staring into the swirling black, I gasped as they started to change. Their faces drooped. The hair fell from their heads in thick tufts. Lizzy's eyes dimmed and appeared to sink into her skull. Her arms pulled in, shrank, disappeared inside her coat.

I stared at her wrinkled, prune-like face—and realized what was happening. I was watching them both age. Watching them age seventy years. Lizzy's mouth fell open, and her teeth dribbled out and fell to the ground. Her skin began to peel. Patches of skin dropped off her forehead, her face, and I could see her cheekbones. She tried to scream but uttered only a hoarse croak.

I uttered a horrified cry as her tongue fell out and hit the cave floor. A pale blob of meat, it wriggled for a few seconds, then went still.

Aaron was now bald and bent over, hands shaking, his body shrunken, skeletal. They were both withered and crumbling. I watched frozen in horror and disbelief. And saw that they didn't stop at old age. As their frail bodies trembled in the swirl of cave wind, their clothes crumpled to the ground. Their bones fell to the cave floor.

Lizzy's face was gone. I gazed at the gaping hole where her teeth and tongue had been. And then the skull toppled off her shoulders and hit the dirt, landing upside down beside her shriveling tongue.

Aaron was a pile of bones now, and the bones were disintegrating, turning to powder. Their bodies were gone. Their bones had slid from their clothes and were noisily cracking and crumbling.

I don't know how long I stood there watching. Was it minutes? Was it just seconds? I watched until Lizzy and Aaron were nothing but ashes, heaps of gray ashes, like at the end of a fireplace fire. And then the swirling cave wind lifted the ashes off the floor and carried them deep into the endless blackness of the cave.

I stared at nothing for a while. And then my brain started to clear, and I remembered Pepper. I remembered Pepper's scream of horror, the scream that had rescued me from the cave, from disappearing in time.

Yes. Yes. Alert now, I remembered Pepper. I forced away the horrifying image of the two people crumbling to ashes. And I started to run, screaming at the top of my lungs, my voice ringing off the trees.

"Pepper? Pepper, are you okay? Pepper?"

46.

I stumbled over a thick pool of leaves, my shoes sliding over the slick snow. "Pepper? Pepper?" My voice, hoarse and desperate, echoed all around.

She turned as I burst through a tangle of trees into the clearing. She squinted at me as if she didn't recognize me.

"Michael?" She stretched her arms, rolled the stiffness from her shoulders. "Michael? What happened? I . . . feel like I was sleeping. But that's impossible. I woke up with a scream and . . ."

"You're okay!" I cried happily. "The spell must have worn off. Thank goodness you're okay."

I wrapped my arms around her and hugged her tight. Her cheeks were frozen. The cold had seeped into her coat, which felt stiff as ice. "You're okay. You're okay." I kept repeating.

I held her for a moment, then backed away. "Pepper, you saved my life. Your scream—it saved me."

She gazed into my eyes. "I feel like . . . I'm waking up

from a nightmare. Where is Lizzy? I remember Lizzy was here. Where did she go?"

"Lizzy is gone. The nightmare is over," I said. "I'll explain everything. But first, let's get out of here." I wrapped my arm around her, and we ran together, out of the dark trees, to the car.

My sheet of paper rattled in the wind. I grabbed it tighter to keep it from blowing away. I saw Pepper and Kathryn near the graveyard fence. They motioned for me to join them, but I waved no. I wanted to be on my own.

It hadn't snowed for two days, and the temperature had risen to nearly forty. Miss Beach announced it was the perfect day to finish our gravestone rubbings.

The morning sun was climbing a clear blue sky. I stepped around some puddles of melting snow and made my way to a marble grave at the end of a row. *Martin Dooley.*

My plan was to do a rubbing of my grandfather's grave and then write a report to go with it of how he came from Ireland as a little boy, worked hard, and soon owned the biggest horse stable in Shadyside. But as I gazed at the words and dates etched in the faded black-and-white marble, I hesitated.

I had too many questions. Was the poor half-blind man really a murderer? Was Grandpa Dooley really the cause of all the horrors my friends and I had just experienced?

I had this crazy idea that he would rise up from the grave. Pull himself up from the snow-covered dirt to explain to me, to say, "No, Michael. I never hurt anyone. I ran the best stable in town, and I loved my family."

A crazy idea. I knew I'd never learn the truth. I would carry all the horror of these past days with me without ever learning the truth.

The wind rattled the paper again. I rolled it up and decided to move on.

Without even realizing it, I had climbed the low hill and was approaching the two Palmieri graves. I could hear the voices of the others in my class, hard at work on their rubbings. They suddenly seemed far away.

I glanced at Angelo Palmieri's grave, then turned to the identical stone beside it. BETH PALMIERI. 1934–1950. I knelt in front of the stone, cold invading the knees of my jeans.

Maybe I'll do a rubbing of her gravestone.

A swirl of wind fluttered my hair, brought a shiver to my back. And over the wind, I heard a whisper, a soft voice that seemed to rise from the ground beneath the gravestone. . . .

"Michael, we're bloods. Remember. We're bloods."

My mouth dropped open. The paper fell from my hand. I jumped to my feet and listened, listened to a cascade of evil laughter, icy like the tinkling of cut glass.